Author's Note

This book is a work of fiction. No character is actual. The subject, Socialism, a dangerous political philosophy, that endures despite its monumental failures throughout its history is real. An untrue philosophy that changes its name to fit the current era. I was born in Cuba and witnessed the destruction that Socialism and its close relative Communism did to a once positively thriving island. I became a naturalized citizen of the United States and served our country as a naval officer. After retiring from the Navy, I worked in the Intelligence Community. I dedicated my adult life to protecting our way of life and our Constitution. I am afraid that Socialism is taking our country into a dangerous end—Globalism. Once entrenched, Globalism will be difficult to remove. Communism, Socialism, Progressivism, and Globalism are interchangeable terms used in this book, and they all mean the same—Centralized Power at the expense of individual freedoms! The stories I portray here are fictional archetypes created from my experience, and research, not actual events.

Dedication

To my parents Estrella y Felo, courage and determination. They came to the United States with only the clothes on their backs; started a new life in their mid-forties. Castro and his henchmen took everything they owned and redistributed their few belongings. They did not speak the English language. They learned a new culture. They succeeded without ever taking a cent from Welfare. They had a superb work ethic, discipline, and belief in God.

To my beautiful daughter, Erica, who does not realize how proud I am of her or how much I love her.

Prologue

After retiring from the Central Intelligence Agency, my grandfather made his home in Beaufort, South Carolina.

My father was a Marine officer. On one occasion, when I was a teenager, he was assigned to Parris Island, Marine Corps Recruiting Depot (MCRD).

I spent long hours with my grandfather. He was a first-rate recontour. I learned to tolerate the hot and humid summer in the Low Country that is Beaufort.

I was sitting in the porch drinking a soft drink while Gramps enjoyed a stronger beverage. He taught me the importance of believing in a supreme being, patriotism, and respecting all people.

My grandfather made sure I was attentive to my schoolwork and surroundings. He said knowledge is the one thing no one can take from you.

When I brought home my textbooks, he would study them with a detective's eye. He was extremely interested in seeing what the school board had approved. He constantly pointed out the importance of the individual in our society. He repeatedly emphasized that the major responsibility of government was to provide for the national defense against all enemies foreign and domestic as well as enforcing the laws of the land equally for all citizens. "Know both sides of an argument," he would say, "that way you will be better prepared to make a sound judgment. Never decide just out of passion, always look at both sides of an argument. Be cautious of envious and deceitful people."

Then, he added, "Government should get out of the way and let the people choose their way to pursuing happiness."

Outside his home, the American Flag proudly flew. As the flag aged due to the effects of weather and time, he would ceremoniously replace it with a new one. The old flag properly folded was then taken to Parris Island Marine Corps Recruiting Depot (MCRD) for proper disposal.

My grandfather emphasized the importance of team sports. So, I played baseball and football. I recognized that in a team sport each player has a job to do and that no one player can do it all. If each player does his job well, there is a good chance that the results will also be good. If one player tries to do it all by either sheer force, anger, or selfish reasons, the results will be bad. I discovered that in life the same is true.

One stifling summer day while cooling off at MCRD pool, I met Erica. She was beautiful. Tall, willowy, smart, and with a terrific sense of humor. She sported a permanent tan that reflected her Mediterranean heritage.

Her father was also a Marine officer. As a child her dad immigrated to the United States from Cuba. His parents sent him to live with his aunt in New York, where he grew up. He became a United States citizen and shortly after graduating from college, he found himself in Quantico, Virginia preparing to earn his second lieutenant butter bar from the Corps.

She told me about her dad growing up in Cuba. They lived in a small two-bedroom house on a dead-end street. How he played a lot of baseball and how he saw on live TV Don Larsen, a New York Yankees pitcher, throw a perfect game against the Brooklyn Dodgers. Her dad told her that all Cuban boys were born with the baseball gene in their DNA and laughed.

Then Castro and his Communist followers took over the country in 1959. Before long, Communism had everyone living in misery. The food was rationed. There were long food lines. People never spoke a word against the government for fear of being thrown in jail. Everyone felt that the streets had ears.

Communism had made everyone equal like they had preached. What they did not advertised was that everyone was equally miserable.

As I got older, I saw how Communism destroyed another prosperous country in Latin America. It took about twenty years for its complete demise. It was Venezuela's turn to experience the agony that is Communism. Once a rich and prosperous country with some of the largest oil reserves in the globe, Venezuelans, like Cubans, fifty years before, now stood in food lines.

As the years went by, and we both got older, the story took different meaning for me. There was one theme, one common denominator, that remained the same—Capitalism trumps Socialism.

PART
1

Chapter

1

I was in the City by the Bay, San Francisco, getting ready to board a Pan American Clipper—destination: the Philippines. It was April of 1940, and the global political climate was reaching a fever pitch. The Spanish Civil War had recently ended, and the Second World War was about to get hotter.

The fear that the Wehrmacht was about to unleash the Blitzkrieg against the West hovered over every European capital. The "Phony War," the quiet eight-month period of limited ground warfare in Western Front at the start of the war, was about to end. In May of 1940, the fear came true, when Germany unleashed its mighty Wehrmacht against France, Belgium, Holland, and England.

The Boeing B-314 was a long-range flying boat. It was one of the largest aircrafts of the time with a powerplant consisting of four Pratt & Whitney radial engines, each capable of 1600 horsepower. The plane carried forty passengers and crew in the overnight sleeper configuration. The elegant brochure described seven luxurious compartments that included a fourteen-seat dining room. Juan Trippe, the owner of Pan American Airlines, did everything first-class, no shortcuts.

It was my first flight on a Clipper, and I looked forward to the adventure before what I would expect to be a stressful stay in Manila.

The main cabin divided into several compartments. The sleeping berths, each with its separate bathroom for men and women, were located towards the rear. Amidships was a comfortable lounge where one could meet other passengers, play cards, relax, or even read a book. Smoking was not allowed inside the aircraft.

The China Clipper, one of the twelve in the Clipper series, was moored midway one of the piers, where seaplanes routinely docked. I took the narrow, covered walkway that led from the terminal to the craft. All the cargo was first loaded and secured in place before the passengers boarded the craft. One last check by a ticket collector who welcomed all passengers and pointed them in the direction to their assigned seats.

The passengers were a mix of businessmen and tourists. We all took our assigned seats, strapped on our seat belts, and did our best to relax before taking off. Suddenly, the door opened, and a well-dressed gentleman entered. He looked about the cabin as if searching for someone. He quickly took his seat, and the crew made the final preparations for takeoff without further delay.

I have a private pilot's license, so in my mind I pictured the activity inside the cockpit. Following the preflight checklist, the pilots, with assistance from the flight engineers, started the engines one by one—all gauges green and ready for departure. Mooring lines were let go by the line-handlers on the pier. The pilots skillfully guided the craft to its water runway.

Throttles pushed forward for maximum power, and the four large engines surged the flying boat forward. First, a slow and noisy roll over the water as it headed into the wind. A little shimmy to the left, a little shimmy to the right, and then straight. As the speed increased, so did the roar of the engines, making conversation impossible, then the aircraft started skipping across the wave tops, creating a spray of water on both sides that was fun to watch. Forty-five seconds later, we were airborne, smooth flying replacing the choppy takeoff.

It was a long flight. The first stage was San Francisco-Honolulu; the second stage, Honolulu-Midway; the third stage, Midway-Wake; the fourth stage, Wake-Guam; and the fifth and final stage, Guam-Manila.

As we gained altitude, the city became smaller and smaller. The Pacific Ocean replaced all human-made structures with its miles and miles of unforgiving blue water. Before long, we were heading west-south-west at a cruising speed of 183 miles per hour while searching for smooth flying air. Above 12,000 feet, oxygen was required to preserve human life; for the entire trip, we flew below that top altitude. The cabin was not pressurized. That technology was not yet available in passenger aircraft.

It felt right to kick back as we flew through broken clouds, looking out the window at the scene below, picking out the wakes of ships as the light thinned away. It was not yet night, but it was no longer day. The next stop was Honolulu, Hawaii, in 2410 miles. The entire trip to Manila was approximately 8200 miles. It would take a whole six days to travel to Manila.

Of those six days, 59 hours and 48 minutes were actually flying. It was time to unwind and maybe get a little shut-eye before dinner service.

I had just sat down to dinner when the gentleman that arrived late for our flight once again showed up. He sat across from me.

He was tall and thin. He looked healthy. His black hair was cropped short, and he had dark eyes close together by the bridge of his nose, like a predator. His dolphin-like lips produced the confident smile of one who thought he was always the smartest man in the room, which often means a lack of self-confidence and insecurity. His swarthy complexion made a good contrast against the light-colored suit he sported.

We made simple conversation during dinner. The stewards cleared the dinner table; the only remaining passengers were the two of us. He invited me to an after-dinner cocktail. The flight steward took our orders, and the stranger said his name was João Sotelo. He was on his way to Hong Kong from Spain. He had been traveling for weeks, first by ocean liner with a stop in New York, a train to San Francisco, and now, finally, in the closing stages of his trip. He looked tired.

We continued our friendly conversation, but never touching on anything significant. Then, a period of sullen silence. It is curious that when two people have been talking, and silence suddenly evolves between them, each person's thoughts go in their direction. Then, upon speaking again, they find how dynamically apart their views have diverged.

Finally, João said that he wished he could smoke. I said that I was sorry, but the rules were no smoking inside the plane. Besides, soon we would arrive in Honolulu, and then he could draw as much as he wished. He gave a guttural sound as if accepting the inevitable. As we exchanged stories, he feigned a smile as if concealing a deep secret. He was born in Santiago de Compostela in northwestern Spain in the province of Galicia. His father was a successful merchant, and he was an only child. João loved order; the study of law seemed inevitable, and he became a lawyer. João's family raised him in the Catholic faith. He was even an altar boy in the Catedral de Santiago de Compostela, completed in 1211 AD. When a student in Salamanca, he traded Catholicism for secularism. When he received his Communist Party Card, he added atheism to secularism.

We had a couple of drinks, and exhaustion finally took the best of us. We retired to our berthing compartments for a well-earned night's sleep after a long tiring day. Only the drone of the four powerful engines filled the cabin.

Chapter

2

We had finished the first stage of our trip. The ground crew resupplied the Clipper with provisions for the journey's next leg: fuel, mail, food, beverages, and fresh linen, among the many requirements. It is very agreeable to find oneself in a beautiful, tropical setting like Honolulu. It gives you an alluring sense of freedom—a good time for the mind to rest.

However, about a year after our stop, on 7 December 1941, that idyllic setting turned into a house of horrors. The Japanese Imperial Navy attacked the United States Navy's most extensive base in the Pacific theater, causing about 3,000 American deaths and crippling a large portion of the Navy's battle fleet.

Suddenly, João, who was sitting adjacent to me, leaned forward and gave me a courtly bow. The booth I was having breakfast in extended on both sides and was decorated with tropical flowers. I was in my own cocoon. I was a bit startled. He must have thought I was either blind or rude for not seeing him.

Again, he invited me over to his table, which I accepted. I asked, "Tell me about Spain?" A deep sigh. "Spain. Things have been a bit rough there during the last few years." He shook his head as if wanting to forget. Silence ensued for a moment as he pondered what to say next. He moved the conversation to a more mundane subject. We talked about the next stage of the trip, and we both wished that it would be as pleasant as the previous one.

Throughout our conversation, I felt that he was concealing a secret, yet he wanted to set free whatever it was that he was suppressing. It is not easy to merge the right facial movements and the particular modulations in voice required to falsify emotions. We shook hands, parted, and prepared for the next stage of the trip.

Chapter

3

We finally found clear flying air at about 8,500 feet on our way to Midway Island, another 1,380 miles. The previous twenty minutes had been unpleasant. We bounced up, down, sideways, forward, and backward while flying through a patch of rough air. Now, operating smoothly, I looked out the window and thanked God that the turbulence was behind us.

João sat near me. He was also looking a bit haggard following the buffeting we had just experienced. He looked out the window at the puffy clouds and the deep blue sea below. I imagined that he was also glad that the harsh flying experience was in the past.

Then, after some meaningless chatter, he asked me my destination. "Manila," I said. That, of course, led to his next question.

"Why Manila?"

"I work for the State Department as a private contractor, and they hired me regarding the purchase of a large building."

"How long will you be there?"

"Only as long as it takes to inspect the building and its surroundings and make a recommendation."

He was satisfied with my answers, for he became quiet and continued to look out the window, but it still seemed as if something was troubling him.

"What was your line of work in Spain?"

He took a moment before answering. His eyes looked up and to the right. I knew this meant he was thinking of something to say that could be fiction. A curious feeling that he was now in hostile territory warned him to keep all his wits about him.

Typically, in Western culture, when asked a question and the person is telling the truth, one will make an eye movement to the left first and then to the right, as if reading since, in Western culture, we read from left to right. Everyone is different, so caution must be taken. His unexpected eye gesture made me raise my pay-attention antenna.

João finally answered that he was a newspaperman and earned his journalism degree from a London university. João spoke perfect English with a British accent.

While a student in Salamanca, João, like many young people in the 1920s and 1930s, was convinced that Communism was the answer to all the world's ills—the triumph of Communism! Here, at last, was the opportunity for total equality. No rich people and no poor people—all equal under the progressive, egalitarian movement. This movement was not peculiar to just Europe.

In America, the intelligentsia led the way on a journey to distance themselves from their social, political, philosophical, cultural, and religious beginnings. It was a time when Communists found their way into the US government to spy for their Soviet handlers; it was an opportunity to influence government policy for Communist goals. Like leopards in the bush, they hid in plain sight, unseen by trusting colleagues.

I thought, "sadly, these turncoat well-to-do Americans failed to see how Communism destroys every man's individuality for the sake of making everyone equally miserable. They fail to see Communism's sinister angle under the watchful of eye of government leaders. The corrupting poison that is power, the disrespectful attitude towards freedom of the press, individual liberty, and the list of rights free people fight for are now under relentless attack under Communism. It's a high price to pay for such 'equality.'"

"By the way, Communism and Socialism are one and the same," said João.

"It is important to use the words appropriately, depending on the audience. Socialism is a softer word, so we use it when trying to recruit. Communism is a hard word, and that's the word we use when among fellow travelers."

João went on to say that the individual is nothing to the Communists. "Individualism meant treason, and it can cost you your life. Communists disdained individualism—free will; the freedom to choose. They discount free will since it means that human beings have the power of independent action. Originality, spontaneity, or any motion originating with the individual is against the benefit of the masses. Everyone is utterly dependent on the total leadership of the few trained administrators qualified to serve the people."

João continued to speak, "a man with freewill may believe in God if he so chooses. Under the Communist yoke, a citizen cannot accept God even if he wants to. Every man, woman, and child, has the capacity for virtue, but that opportunity is negated. This is my good deed—that I love beauty, which pleases me wholeheartedly; I only desire to do good, but Communism prohibits that opportunity also. Instead, ordinary people are herded into lives of suffering and hunger, the two inevitable results that Communism so richly redistributes."

I felt that I was getting a graduate lesson in Communism. I had read about what had transpired in Russia after the Revolution of 1917. I knew that the Soviet nomenklatura lived in privilege while the rest of the people wore rags. But what I was learning from João was so much more.

João, the teacher, and I, the student.

After listening to my new teacher, I thought, "that Communism is missing key elements that make life worthwhile—namely, the idea of liberty, the means of acquiring and owning property, and pursuing happiness and safety. Good governance allows for the common benefit and security for the people. An excellent government provides opportunities; it does not smother or stifle them. It allows for the primacy of the individual over the government in moral authority. It follows that the great enemy of liberty, of individual liberty, is government. The government tends to encroach upon the innate freedoms of the individual."

João told me that as part of his training, he and the others in the class of recruits were taught about the meaning of Liberalism versus Socialism. He said that "in the eighteenth century, Liberalism stressed individual rights and a self-regulating market. Today, Liberalism means community rights and government market regulations. It is no coincidence that under Communism, social problems are in proportion to government intervention and intrusion in people's lives. This sad circumstance is the result of the unnecessary excessive growth of government administration. It then becomes inevitable that life will be short and miserable. A hungry person neither listens to reason nor is mollified or swayed by false appeals."

He continued, "for a Communist system to remain in power, it must depend on a political police as well as a secret police. A Communist government cannot allow free expression of public discontent. During a Communist revolution, newspapers must be eliminated or at least controlled. A revolution cannot have a free press. The only way it can succeed is by suppression. The result is terrible economics, corruption, and totalitarianism.

John Locke's ideas regarding the individual do not agree with Communist views. Locke said, in his book *The First and Second Treatise of Government*, "To understand political power right, and derive it from its original, we must consider, what state all men are naturally in, and that is, a state of perfect freedom orders their actions, and dispose of their possessions and persons, as they see fit, within the bounds of the law of nature, without asking leave, or depending upon the will of any other man."

João finally earned his Communist Party card. He also learned that no one ever leaves the party of his own accord without repercussions. He heard rumors about assassination teams and cruel emissaries with long memories. The secret organization regarding assassination operations was kept by careful selection of agents, who received specialized training. All assassins were trained in the art of hit-and-run tactics and kidnapping. The target list was long. High-ranking, influential Communist apostates highlighted the top of the list.

At this stage of training, he had displayed loyalty, high energy, and, most importantly, a gift for words. Party leaders decided to send him to London to earn his journalism degree. It was while he was a student in London that he got his first taste of spying. He was successful in recruiting a couple of inexperienced and idealistic classmates. Like so many young, privileged men of that time, these two could not wait to do their best to advance the triumphs of Communism. They would pay dearly in the future and were disillusioned with their choice of political philosophy. For now, João had identified talent for the cause, a valuable instinct. His handlers liked this small but telling accomplishment. It was the start of a new career.

Party leaders told him that one day, he would become an agent of influence. Agents of influence fell into several categories. He liked that phrase; it sounded important. Agents of influence were individuals who could shape policy or public opinion, organize political operations, and even create and fund front groups for the cause.

He did not become a journalist by choice. The Party had chosen that path for him, and he willingly followed orders.

He was speaking slowly as if he was thinking out what to say next. He possessed the good, heady power of finding the proper words to express his thoughts, his ideas. His voice was soft, and his enunciation was clear as a bell. "The Soviet's intelligence service, NKVD, prioritized the recruitment of agents of influence. These individuals included journalists, and that was the primary reason the Soviets had financed my schooling in London. Journalists penned editorials and were in a position to shape public opinion in a way that favored the Soviet Union."

João continued describing how journalists shape public opinion. "The opposition's positive news was omitted, under-reported, or completely modified. For example, good economic news was downplayed by saying that all people were not bene-fitting and that only a particular group was prospering. It is not what you say, but how you say it."

João further stated ways that one can identify the recruit-ment of talent. He said that he was taught that there are four main principles for recruitment. There was a simple acronym to remember, MICE: Money, Ideology, Coercion, and Ego. They were taught to be on the lookout for an influential man's weakness. One that can be snared and manipulated. He further said that potential assets come in categories: recruited, en-trapped, and blackmailed.

"The recruited," he said, "are genuine followers or walk-ins are substantial assets, for the most part. They form the most highly valued sources since those who gave information for ideological reasons required no payment. They risk their life, reputation, and, if unmasked, do not give up secrets.

"The entrapped are ready to do almost anything for money, and usually do good work, but cannot be trusted. Their loyalty lies with whoever is willing to pay. If caught, the asset will prob-ably try to change sides or surrender secret information in re-turn for his liberty."

"The blackmailed assets do our dirty work—many who were found in flagrante delicto with members of the opposite or same-sex fall under this category. Blackmailed men will do as told. They are afraid that exposing 'skeletons in the closet' may reveal their secret life to the public and tarnish their 'up-right and moral' reputation."

When João finished telling me this information, I was completely confused and at the same time a bit scared. There are many ways to get someone to betray one's country. I had not thought about all the different angles one can become a traitor. But João was not finished with his lesson in Spying 101. He continued, "Now the NKVD becomes deeply involved in 'active measures,' which fundamentally means dirty tricks and disinformation. Also, active measures include the infiltration of the opposition's organizations, colleagues, and finances. Planted stories are regularly employed that describe the opposition as racist and misogynous and detail any other despicable act that leads to their downfall. The active measure does not discriminate based on creed, race, or color. Everything is fair game. It does not matter who or what is destroyed along the way."

By this time, I was really concerned about the way Communists trained their assets. These people were experts and their ability to possibly infiltrate into every institution in our country. I was concerned and felt I had to do something to prevent, or at least slow down the red tide.

Chapter

4

After a silent period, João continued with his lesson in Spying 101. "Propaganda is not enough to accomplish the Socialist's goals. *Agent provocateurs* are recruited to spread lies, half-truths, and innuendos to a much wider audience. They are planted among malcontent and radical organizations. They are embedded in government offices, politicians' homes, businesses; in fact, anywhere influential people gather is the right place for one of these agents to reside.

"They cynically ask, 'don't you care about the life and suffering of our fellow human beings?' If you deceive and lie to the people, you are now conditioned to repeat it again and again.

"Propaganda attacks people's morale by promoting defeatism. The purpose is to deliver truths mixed with half-truths, false rumors, and deliberate libels dropped on people that have done nothing wrong. Propaganda spreads like wildfire, like the flu into every unsuspecting home. Since the average person believes most easily what they want to think, propaganda must always be directed to stir emotion. People half-informed are eager to hear more and are easy targets for the distributors of propaganda to reach innocent and unsuspecting people."

I felt that João was giving me a lesson in real life. Maybe it was because up to this time I had lived a sheltered life. I was relatively young and inexperienced in world affairs. All I really knew was book learning, but in many cases, what we learn in the classroom does not transfer into real-life events. Failure in the classroom means a lower grade. Failure in world affairs could mean death.

He continued with his monologue. "Most European governments for the last ten to fifteen years represented the will of the people. They promoted slums, unemployment, and condone a cowardly foreign policy." He pointed the finger at the British and French appeasers that stiffened the spines of Mussolini and Hitler.

On he went. "You see, Communists are the preachers of death. They are shrouded in deep melancholy awaiting death because, for them, life is only suffering. Their hearts are filled with envy and hate. This is the moment where the domineering man meets the meek, the suffering, the forgotten, and they completely misunderstand each other. Communists give the impression that failure and weakness are more delicate and a more noble act than success and strength.

I read newspapers, magazines, and scholarly publications like *Foreign Affairs*. Up to that time I believed that the authors and publishers of those publications were politically neutral. That their intention was to inform the public and not to recruit them into their political beliefs. I know now that was a naïve position. From my readings I knew that the 1930s was a stagnant period led by mediocre leaders that allowed fertile ground for Socialist recruitment, but I did not pay enough attention to what was happening because I was trying to find my own way in the world. I should have known that when problems are left unattended, they have a habit of becoming a crisis. João was opening my eyes to a world I did not know.

João now continued with lessons in Communism and Socialism. "Everyone allocated a fixed source of income that came from an unknown origin: a salary, a retirement pension, student aid, but always supplied by the government. Your freedom to choose—removed. Extra earnings were prohibited; no one could legally make money on the side, which, of course, promoted the black market where products were available for the right price."

"Redistribution of wealth and social justice was now the new Socialist's slogan. Let's not forget 'Internationalism,'—the dream that one day the entire globe would be a Leninist, Marxist, Communist paradise with 'The Internationale' as the global anthem, replacing all other hymns."

"If everyone were to seize for himself the advantages other men have and take what he could for himself, indeed fellowship among men would be destroyed. Redistribution of wealth is so morally wrong. An untouchable administrator gives away what is not his to give away in the first place. It is political stealing, which is always corrupt.

"The judge asks, 'Why did this man commit murder?' Response: 'Oh, he meant to rob, your honor.' Socialists and their redistribution of wealth cause is all about stealing; it is all about snatching until there is nothing else to nab. To take revenge against the hard-working people that earned their way to prosperity via hard work, discipline, and belief in a higher being.

"Those in power should refrain from actions like redistribution of wealth, but the Socialist politician has no conscience, just lust for power.

"Socialism is a disease that reaches into a man's soul, preying on his weaknesses and paralyzing his reason and beliefs. The good in people becomes their downfall, while evil is exalted. Truth, fidelity, and justice do not matter in this corrupt political system.

"Justice is justice and does not need a modifier. Social justice is injustice. Justice is the moral disposition that makes men do just things. Justice is lawful, which is equal and fair. Justice stands alone and does not require a conditioner. Beware of future modifiers before the word justice.

"Injustice applies to the lawbreaker and the man who takes more than his share. It means that which is illegal, unequal, and unfair. If a man is knowingly acting in a way that will result in his actions being unjust, he is willingly unjust and untrustworthy. In many cases, this is the very definition of a politician or an unelected government administrator.

"When politicians ruin the community by taking away one's property, they will not achieve what they think they will, for a man or woman whose property has been stolen will be hostile. The one who receives it pretends not to want it; however, all his debts are forgiven, and he hides his joy. Therefore, justice must be cultivated and preserved by all methods.

"International solidarity is a pipe dream. Nationalism reigns supreme in every corner of the globe. People always identify with a family, a clan, a region, a flag, a country. Only the 'International intelligentsia' believes in one peaceful international community. One needs to ask which region, state, or person is the head of the global government? Where is the world capital going to be located? Is it Washington DC, Moscow, London, Berlin, Peking, or maybe a new location, like Wuhan, China? Will the leaders of Bolivia or Egypt be the supreme leader one day, or does supreme leadership only belong to the powerful like China, Russia, Great Britain, and the United States?

"This mad trinity now represented the Socialist way forward. Forget about ethics and doing right by the citizens. The entire Socialist leadership and its support forces are sailing without ethical ballast in the presence of such thoughts; traditional morality fails."

He continued to confess as his voice quivered with anger, and his hands rolled up into a fist. "It may take generations, but eventually, these repeated false promises will become a reality since we Socialists play the long game—patient to a degree. We've had to survive the world's reaction to our policies. The Socialist camp must continue to stand until the world is ready for a new wave of revolution. They stand alone, and their only duty is to survive and not to perish, which means opposing patriotism, disrupting the family unit, and, finally, once and for all, burying God.

"History has no conscience. So, it only follows that we do not deliberate about the ends, but about the means. The end of religion and the rise of secularism. The first step is control of the education system: secular education and the end of nationalism. Teach the children our Socialist's ways from the very beginning when the mind and habits are malleable."

João's voice lowered almost as if speaking in a whisper, his head shook from side to side, and he raised his shoulders and hands in despair. He said, "How long can you fool people with false promises built on deceitful wet sand and not a dry foundation of truth before they realize they been hoodwinked? Hopefully people will see through this mirage just like I did. Anyway, my outlook on Socialism was turning dusky, not yet dark, but making me think twice about the path I had taken.

"As a lawyer, I was taught the following: 'When fighting a case, if you have the facts on your side, hammer them into the jury. If you have the law on your side, hammer it into the judge. However, if you have neither the facts nor the law, then hammer the table into hell with your fists.' That is what the Socialists do. They angrily repeat the same vicious lies until the lies become the truth."

João's revelation left him with a strangely haunted look. He was agitated and extremely nervous. He was notably emotional—an appeal to the heart and not the mind.

I now understood that the Socialist propaganda machine feeds the newspapers with lies, half-truths, and innuendos.

João moved forward in his role as an agent of influence. He was proud of his work until he saw through the veil of Socialist corruption designed to keep the party elites, the nomenklatura, in power, while the people they were supposed to protect fell into a bottomless pit of despair.

João and I continued our conversation while munching on snacks and drinking red wine. His instructors said, "Know, understand, and believe that the ends, certainly, justify the means. As a correspondent of a Communist paper, it is necessary to lie. With time, with experience, you will develop that technique of lying. It will become innate. You will protect the dishonest actions of those on your side and virulently attack your enemies even when no malicious acts have been committed. Eventually, in good faith, it will have no meaning. When self-deception becomes routine, it ceases to be an excuse. It ceases to be a problem. So, we filled newspapers with disturbing bluster and peril of such swindle; set it before the public, not as lies, but as news.

"The real role of a leading journalist is not just in the next opinion, but also to shape it—most importantly, when a significant opponent rests on shaky assumptions. It is not the role of newspaper editors to suppress news because it might prevent it from achieving their intended goals."

We took a break from this depressing talk, but it was not long before João said, "One day, I'm walking in a town when I stumble into a conversation between two men. 'In a Socialist state, we should be richly pensioned.'

"'Don't talk to me about your Socialists,' said the second man; 'I've got no patience with them. It only means another lot of lazy loafers will make a good thing out of the working classes. My motto is to leave me alone. I don't want anyone interfering with me. I'll make the best of a bad situation, but I am my own man. Don't want the government's help that comes with so many strings attached. They giveth, but just as easily taketh away.'

"After listening to this conversation, I thought there might be hope for humanity."

João continued to speak. "Life in a Communist-controlled country made it imperative to pretend to believe in the ideology that promised a rosy future. That was far from the reality of daily life. To survive, one has to use cunning, lying, and masquerade." He spoke as if wittingly withholding information, not by accident. He wore a forced smile, and his voice became softer and lower while the corners of his eyebrows were raised.

He appeared tortured by the desire to reveal some huge secret. João had the look of a man who had been in hell and witnessed hopeless suffering, lying, and meanness. It was as if he were reflecting on whether his adult life had been a worthless quest. This agent of influence was an unhappy man.

João made no secret of the fact that Marxist-Leninists looked upon their fellow men as fools and scamps. He continued his confession: "Marxists want to blow up society, no matter the consequences and suffering it may bring. They take advantage of people's envy and jealousy. They know that in many communities, the poor despise respectable men, wealthy or not; it does not matter. They exalt the rotten, they detest tradition and call for change because of the circumstances they have put themselves in by making poor choices. They feast on turmoil and treason. They do not care about the consequences because they have nothing to lose."

I was suspicious and in awe of João at the same time. Was he testing a new recruiting pitch on me? Was he telling the truth? Did he sense that I was much more than a government contractor? If so, did he see me as a new recruit that could work for his cause from inside the United States government? A million thoughts whirled in my head in a nanosecond.

After what he had told me, I was not sure what to believe. I knew this much, however. I would listen to him as long as he talked, but I was not going to divulge my beliefs to this guy. I continued acting like I was interested in his story, which I was. I continued acting like an inexperienced young man, which I was. And I refused to act like the most intelligent person in the room. I needed to be ready to fight back the red tide.

My fear was the possible spread of this malignant political ideology into our country. João did not stop at the personal attacks that Socialism would bring into a society. He then went on to describe that rabid Socialist just do not like anything except their own ideas.

He said, "Socialists violate art, architecture, literature, music, or anything of exceptional beauty. They find it disgusting since they believe that it slanders the extraordinary man. They claim art exists because it promotes beauty—a capitalist habit. It is how capitalists keep you looking in the wrong direction while they exploit the people."

I pondered how often, during our lives, we seek evil and fall into it with open arms. We descend into a bog of calumny and wallow in its embrace for a time until we are wholly consumed by its putrefying filth. It is a dreadful situation, but frequently, it is also our means of deliverance. We can overcome, raise ourselves from the affliction we have fallen into. This is what I felt as João spoke. João found his salvation from the cynical world of Socialism.

João's speech was now fast and emphatic, and his nervous manner made me nervous too. "Violence, if necessary, is a method to plant Marxism in society, and it requires co-opting the intelligentsia, industry, the armed forces, and the police.

"During one of my political indoctrination sessions, a high-ranking deputy prime minister said: 'The British Labor government is 'fascists' for two reasons. They have not filled the British Army with Socialist generals, and they have not taken over Scotland Yard.' It was easy to recognize that Socialists must infiltrate a country's armed forces, the government, law enforcement, the judicial, and all governmental functions.

"He had reasons for his anger against the English and told us about successes in America. He described how the most crucial intelligence tool involved the use of informers and moles. A mole provokes mistrust. He undermines coherent belief.

A mole's primary targets for penetration included the White House, Congress, State Department, the military, leading scientific research centers, essential think tanks, and even major corporations. The White House, he said, 'is already infiltrated by senior assistants and deputy cabinet members. Journalists, famous authors, and editors of influential publishers are already helping our cause. I have names, but I do not want to expose them to any danger. We back our helpers with the aid of *active measures*—a new term for my vocabulary—spreading disinformation and stirring trouble within disenfranchised minorities.'"

When João finished telling me all this, I was nervous about the future of my country. Would Socialism infiltrate our shores and take hold? I was rightfully concerned and felt it was time to act. The question was: how can I help? I knew that, in the short-term, the United States was headed for war. Japan was quickly beating the drums of war in the Far East. Germany was not satisfied with her gains in eastern Europe. It was quite apparent to me that, in the long-term, the Soviet Union did not respect borders. The Russian bear was looking where to strike next. The world was about to become more dangerous and complicated. Soon I discovered an avenue to fight back against Socialism—or maybe I should say, an avenue discovered me.

João continued, "The Russian people never do anything they do not want to do. They condone almost anything and only tolerate other people's ideas to a small degree, which brings me to this question: Why do Russians spend so much time with problems, such as man's destiny? They have never produced a first-rate philosopher. It is as if they don't have the capacity for profound thought.

"Yes, in the last one hundred and fifty years, they have produced great novelists like Pushkin, Gogol, Lermontov, Turgenev, Tolstoy, Dostoevsky, Chekov, Gorky, all passionate writers. But not one philosopher like: Plato, Aristotle, Immanuel Kant, Friedrich Nietzsche, David Hume, John Locke, and so many others. "Russian literature, although passionate, it is also pessimistic. It seems that all books promote the same theme. Russians suffer in their early years. Middle-age means more foolish suffering. They blame czarism, they blame women, they blame a successful neighbor, and they blame the universe for their failures. In old age, they become aware of all the mistakes they made during their lives. Now that death is lurking around the corner, the blame is again cast at persons, places, or things, but never at themselves, who are the responsible actors for their own sorry lives."

I thought about João's remarks. It reminded me of a *Bible* passage from *The New King James Version, Book of Genesis (3:9-14)*: "After the man, Adam, had eaten of the tree, the Lord God called the man and asked him, where are you?

He answered, I heard you were in the garden, but I was afraid because I was naked, so I hid.

Then he asked, who told you that you were naked? You have eaten, then, from the tree of which I had forbidden you to eat!"

The man replied, the woman whom you put here with me—she gave the fruit from the tree, and so I ate it.

The Lord then asked the woman, why did you do such a thing? The woman answered, the serpent tricked me into it, so I ate it."

Here we have the very first attempted coup d'état. It reminded me of all the Socialist promises for a better life, when in reality their promises bring death and despair. Thankfully the Lucifer's attempted coup d'état failed, just like any future Socialist attempt at taking over our government by false promises.

It was easy to blame others for your own sorry lives; never, ever, accept that you are the one responsible for your actions. It is always someone else's fault that you are mired in quicksand. Very similar to what Socialists always say when their ideas go awry—it is the capitalists' fault!

I have since learned that Christianity was the main reason why the West was powerful. More important than guns, was the Christian moral foundation of social and cultural life and the reason why the West had been prosperous to transition to Democratic politics. Christianity provides a moral code—God's law.

We all fail to achieve the Ten Commandments' standards, but one can always try to approach them and clear the soul from its sinful stain. We call this act "redemption," and it allows us to seek a better path.

Secularism is only concerned with the body, not the soul. Live for today, for there is no afterlife. Secularism's moral code is empty of truth; its cargo holds filled with evil passions. Evil passions become its virtues, and devils become its angels.

Socialists fomented the growing skepticism of religion and specific attacks against Christianity by Socialist philosophers that provided the intellectual position. This was another reason the Left was in an all-out war against religion. God was dead!

Secularism is the way forward. This stance supported proposals to increase the power of the state over the church. It also provided the opportunity to create a sort of state religion that was deemed necessary for public order and the adaptation of new moral standards. The agents of influence moved forward this falsehood with identical newspaper articles and press releases. As we sat on the flying boat's comfortable lounge, I continued to reflect on what João had said. The droning of the engines engulfed the cabin as I looked out the window at the distant horizon and seemed to put a spell over me. I fell asleep. After the catnap, a crewmember asked if we would like to come forward to the cockpit and take a look around. We were overwhelmed by the numerous gauges and dials that required constant attention to maintain safe flight. The telegraph crackled with the distinct sound of dits and dots as weather reports arrived.

The view before us had no beginning and no end. Now the horizon seemed even farther away. Flying through transparent clouds provided the reference of speed. All in all, it was an exhilarating adventure for the two of us. I felt like I was piloting the plane. Now I needed to pilot my life.

Following our brief adventure in the cockpit, we returned to the lounge and ordered drinks. As I sat comfortably in my seat, I could not help but think of what João had explained to me during our many conversations. I boiled it down to simple explanation. The Socialists brew a political poison, it is marketed for all to see; and then, the people are forced to drink the poison. One way or the other, they will perish, either through Socialist coercion, or their souls so fraught with venom that they die in solitude and despair.

The more cynosure the man, the harder he works on becoming a politician. His rhetoric leads the average person to believe that they must prepare for the great struggle against oppression. They make the people suffer greatly for a cause they do not fully understand.

João described the true revolutionary man as a humorless person with an unshakable belief in social justice and who renounces all life's pleasures to work for the happiness of humanity. As João pronounced, "happiness" and "humanity," his nose wrinkled with intensity while his eyebrows were pulled down, a sure sign of disgust. He knew that caring for humanity's happiness was only a slogan. The reality was that "humanism" is utterly alien to the Socialist's sense of right and wrong.

João continued his story regarding his training in Moscow. He said, "The instructors told us, 'Comrades, we are going to infiltrate our enemy. We will co-opt their politicians and journalists. The latter is where all of you will play your key roles. We want you to camouflage your ideas, but only for a short time. Once we are rolling with our way of doing things, we will not bother about the heart of the people.'"

As he finished his thought, we encountered another pocket of turbulent air. We went down rapidly and then up just as quickly before continuing smooth flying—like floating on a calm river. We both had white-knuckle grips on the armrests. We looked at each other and smiled with a sigh of relief.

Chapter

5

João was a member of a group of foreigners visiting Russia in late 1936. They were all VIPs rewarded by Moscow's elite for their loyalty and excellent work in promoting Socialist ideals. He saw the future during a visit to a model collective and was completely disillusioned. He said, "All the homes were uniformly depressing. There was a total absence of individuality. Cheap ugly furniture accented only by a smiling picture of Stalin. There was nothing personal. All the houses are the same. Commonality once again adorned even glorified each home. It was all a symbol mendacity."

I interrupted João for a bit of clarification and asked him, "If most people living under these conditions had any regrets of supporting Socialism?"

He said that "there was not much that people could do without getting harsh punishment. If they protested, they had a guaranteed one-way ticket to Siberia. Never to be heard of again."

I thought, is this any way to live? Does anyone want to be fed and housed by the government? Socialism provides the basics for living, but for a high price—your blind loyalty. Instead, I wanted to be a free man. I choose things because I wanted to adopt them and not because the government tells what I can and cannot do.

João felt that the Russians he spoke with said that "the government fails to realize that most people do not want to be corralled like obedient sheep. They are not animals, they are not stupid, and they don't wish to exist merely. Instead, they want to live as intelligent decision-makers, diligent, and creative people. We want to be free to succeed or fail on our terms. However, the government sets the standards, and you better live by them, or you become feed for persecution."

João continued: "Wherever you go, there is only one opinion. *Pravda* and *Izvestiia*, the government-run newspapers, tells the people all they need to know, what to believe, and what to think. A set of journalists collects lies, and a second set scatters them and a third distributes them to the public as truths. In a country where all publications are state-run, editors, publishers, and critics become puppets of the state's media. There is nothing sacred about theories. They serve only as instruments."

I sat back and listened as João continued to speak. "Socialists try to make everything too definite, and that is a significant error. They try to place everything in a neat box. 'A' goes in the 'A Box,' and 'B' goes in the 'B Box,' and so on. Life does not work like that. People have goals and dreams.

"What hurt the most was the absence of mention of the Spanish Civil War in any newspaper. While at a sumptuous dinner, by Bolshevik standards, I proposed a toast to the triumph of the

Red cause and the International Brigades fighting alongside the Loyalists—the Madrid government. The company applauded with caution and a lack of intimacy. The reason for the lack of enthusiasm? The *Pravda* editors had not made an official pronouncement on the Spanish question.

"It turns out that the casualty rate for the International Brigades was astronomical. Two-thirds of the foreign fighters met their deaths during the civil war. The Communist International (COMINTERN) created and controlled International Brigades. The rank and file consisted mainly of Communists and sympathizers from all corners of the globe. Only party members were allowed in leadership roles and were directly responsible for the Communist Party apparatus."

João told me how, "at the very beginning of the rebellion, the Spanish government decided to take advantage of its friendship with the French government. José Giral, the Spanish prime minister, telegraphed the French leadership to ask for arms and ammunition. Spain had vast gold reserves of about $600,000,000—at that time, substantial negotiating leverage.

"Concurrently, they negotiated to buy weapons from the Russians. They felt that they would be willing to deal with them quickly, although furtively because of fear getting caught red-handed selling weapons now that the major powers had signed the Non-Intervention Pact. At first, Stalin stalled the sales. The Spanish government could not understand how a country that claimed to be the protector of Socialism failed to supply them with weapons. In the meantime, Germany and Italy openly equipped their enemy with modern weapons. This action should have raised a big red flag regarding Soviet loyalty to our cause, but I failed to see it.

"Russians were now in a position to dictate terms for the weapons sale since Communist parties of every country had to carry out Russian policy. In Spain during the civil war, the terms meant the prevention of revolution or no weapons. The anarchists, certain Socialist groups, and any group that did not embrace Communism as the first and only legitimate form of government had to be eliminated.

"After several weeks of hesitation, Russian negotiators finally informed the Spanish leadership that they were ready to sell them weapons as long as they paid in cash. The Spanish government fed the Russians in gold.

"Finally, some equipment arrived in the port of Cartagena: a few tanks and light artillery. In November, another Russian vessel off-loaded its cargo in the port of Alicante. The Russian equipment was obsolete, and the Loyalists had paid not only in gold but also in blood. Many rifles dated back to the Crimean War. A half a dozen airplanes, twelve light tanks, and fifty machine guns were delivered—a disgrace by all standards. The Russians did not act like the right defenders of a small Socialist ally."

João was almost crying when he finished talking.

João went on to explain that "Soviet aid to the Loyalists, after reaching a maximum in December 1936, gradually diminished through 1937. By now, I'm thinking that they had never considered aiding us in the long run. It was all about their survival. In August of 1939, it all became clear as a full moon on a cloudless night—Stalin and Hitler agreed to a non-aggression pact—the Molotov-Ribbentrop Pact. A few weeks later, after Poland surrendered to the Germans, Hitler and Stalin carved up Poland. Hitler took the western half, and Stalin took the eastern half.

"I was thunderstruck as if awakened from a bad dream. Now I had doubts about the cause we fought. I knew that we were just a pawn to be used and discarded when the time was right.

"I wrongly believed that we were all fighting, together, for a better world—an egalitarian society and that we all had a voice in shaping our 'international' world. Make everyone equal. Abolish fear, envy, greed, and stupidity. The facts proved me wrong.

"No single person was allowed to think on his own. The red law, which is not law, commanded that everyone blindly, strictly followed the dictum of the Communist Party or face shame, resentment, incarceration, or worse. You see, they believe that a representative government is essentially a government by a man instead of law. Active political responsibility is in the hands of those 'elected' party officials. What follows are long food lines, secret police, and a complicit media telling you what and how to think."

João said, "People can make mistakes, but the Party is never wrong. The Party is so much more than a flock of its followers. The Party represents the historical revolutionary idea, and history does not dither; it is always moving in cadence with time. Moderates are not allowed in the Party, for it is they who often betray progress with their good intentions."

Then, João said, "It wasn't only the Russians who were either dishonest or just plain stupid. A meeting was set to defend a small but strategically important island in the Mediterranean Sea. As the military leaders discussed the resupplying of the island with men and equipment, the political commissar started posing questions like a newly minted lawyer. Almost illiterate, and of a swarthy complexion, eyes set far apart like a fish, and he spoke slowly as if the words only reach his brain after much hard work."

"He said, 'Well, wouldn't the island tip over and sink if you put all that equipment and men?' The attendants at the meeting flabbergasted by this ignorant comment; they did not know whether to laugh or cry. With cretins like this political hack, the war was going to be a long one. First, we have to defeat the enemy, and then we have to overcome fools inside the government.

"On another defensive perimeter, we were building a wall to protect our soldiers and to prevent further incursion by the enemy. A tall, slow-witted woman opposed building the wall. She possessed big hands like a 'cesta,' a long, curved wicker scoop strapped to one arm of a jai alai player.

"She said, 'Why don't you cut the grass so that you can see when they are coming?' That way it will be easier to kill them.

"Again, we thought, there is no way we can win this war when we have moron politicians."

His voice was hoarse with emotion. Sometimes, as if he were ashamed of what he was saying, he spoke with his eyes fixed on the floor. His face was distorted with pain, yet I believed he felt a strange sense of relief. In the end, he laughed out loud at the ignorance of the politicians on his side.

Chapter

6

Who could have predicted that the island of Midway would be the site of one of the great naval battles in history, comparable to Salamis, Trafalgar, and Tsushima Strait? The Battle of Midway was a decisive naval battle during World War II. It took place between 4 and 7 June 1942, just two short years after my stop there on my way to Manila. Six months after the Japanese attack on Pearl Harbor, the two major naval powers in the Pacific Ocean, Japan and the United States, faced off.

The Japanese Navy suffered a great defeat that was inflicted by the United States Navy. The Imperial Japanese Navy never fully recovered. They had lost hundreds of experienced irreplaceable pilots and the king of their fleet, aircraft carriers.

I was reading a Pan Am magazine in the lobby of pleasant hotel in Midway. It told the story of how Juan Trippe, Pan American Airline's owner, took on the challenge of making flying across the Pacific Ocean a reality. The article described how flying over the Pacific presented a much bigger challenge than crossing the Atlantic. Just the distance from San Francisco to Honolulu was about 2,400 miles. When Pan American's planners began thinking of crossing the Pacific, the most extended leg the airlines flew was under 600 miles.

The real obstacle to a route across the Pacific was the distance between Midway and Guam. Desperate to put his plans to work for crossing the vast ocean, Juan Trippe looked for a solution. His search revealed the strategic location of a small, uninhabited Pacific island named Wake. Claimed by the US in 1899, but deserted and virtually forgotten, Wake was just 1,200 miles from Midway and within reach of Guam—the perfect stepping-stone to cross the vast Pacific.

Before Pan Am could begin flying the Pacific, however, it needed to develop operating bases. Wake Island was uninhabited, and neither Midway nor Guam had facilities to support Pan American's aircraft, passengers, crew, navigation, and weather equipment.

Early in 1935, Pan Am leased a freighter, North Haven. The ship's cargo holds were loaded with all the items required for operations— matériel for buildings, construction equipment, boats, and long-distance direction-finding equipment. Additionally, a four-month supply of food, aviation fuel, and some 120 laborers, engineers, demolition experts, and other workers aided in making the island operational.

While construction was in progress, Pan Am experts concurrently made their first Pacific Ocean survey flights. Finally, with the precise surveys completed and the routes identified and deemed safe for travel, Trippe was ready to see a financial return for his investment. On October 21, 1936, the Hawaiian

Clipper left San Francisco with the first-ever paying customers to cross the Pacific Ocean by air.

I felt pretty special; only four years after the initial flight, I was one of the passengers flying over the Pacific Ocean. I finished the article and looked out the window, my mind replaying the conversation with João the day before.

Our talk made me think of Sisyphus, the king of Ephyra. The Greek gods punished him for his self-promotion craftiness and deceitfulness, forcing him to roll a boulder up a hill only for it to roll down when it neared the top. Socialism destines the average person to become a modern-day Sisyphus, intended to work without reward.

The Left's leadership reminded me of Socialists gods that condemned their citizens to absolute misery. They get to improve their lot by deceitfully promising a better life for all. The people suffer while the leadership lives comfortably.

Keep pushing the boulder uphill.

People should be critical and not accept solutions that have not materialized for problems that have. In a healthy society, those in leadership roles should behave justly, like the laws they make. They should be fair to all and not punish people because they are in charge or angry. Among free people who possess equality before the law, we must cultivate civil temperament. Unfortunately, we all know that this is only a dream. It is not that anyone imagines the rules to be fair. Everyone knows that there is one law for the rich and powerful and another for the rest of us.

Nothing is more dishonorable than falsehood. There is zero honor in Socialism, for honor requires learning, sociability, moderation, and, most importantly, a noble spirit.

Beware of the desire for glory, which is one of the characteristics of a deceitful politician. He is often one struggling for a position of honor when he does not possess an ounce of that virtue. His actions are, in fact, an altogether wretched practice. Too often, these politicians emerge in public life as agitators or bribers, seeking wealth and preferring violent deceit to equality through justice.

Morality and religion are like a hand to a glove: they fit together as one. If you lose faith, virtue stays behind. A man is more likely to be a good man if he has learned righteousness through the love of God rather than by reading Marx.

My musings came to an end when a Pan Am messenger boy said that passengers would be boarding the Clipper for the next leg of the trip, Wake Island, in two hours. The meteorologists predicted good flying weather for the next day. I prepared for boarding.

Chapter

In December 1941, Wake Island, this peaceful and tiny island would become a modern-day Alamo as a handful of Marines and civilian workers fought against the Imperial Japanese Navy's invasion. American resistance against Rear Admiral Sadamichi Kajioka was savage. With a force comprised of a light cruiser, six destroyers, two transport ships, and a landing party of 560 trained sailors, the invaders were thrown back into the sea.

Standing between Japanese victory and failure were 250 Marines and 100 civilian workers led by Major James Devereux, USMC. Some of the civilians worked for Pan American Airlines. The Wake defenders held out to the last bullet but eventually surrendered to the vastly superior Japanese invading force.

We were flying smoothly to Wake a mere 1,260 miles away. We both had peaceful smiles on our faces after a couple of cocktails. We were flying nice and smooth with no excitement; it was not like the previous leg, which had resembled a roller-coaster ride.

I was glued to every word he said when he started talking about Stalin's purges of the mid-1930s. He said that "past loyal actions no longer counted under Stalin. The arrests came in connection against a large group of mythical conspirators. Another set of unidentified mythical leaders supposedly were led by the Promparty and the Union Bureau. Stalin and his cohorts imagined plots everywhere. People lived in fear of a midnight knock on the door by the dreaded secret police who came with a one-way ticket to the Lubyanka prison.

"Sometime around 1935 or 1936," said João, "the old Bolsheviks that played a significant role in the 1917 revolution stood accused in a series of show trials. Government prosecutors made outrageous claims. They were accused of treasonous activities: counter-revolutionary acts espionage, and even plots to overthrow the Soviet regime. The heroes of the 1917 revolution felt impotent and cowered before the mountain of lies and half-truths shot at them by immoral prosecutors."

As I listened to João's story, I become more alarmed at the possibility of Socialism finding its way to the United States. I felt that the key to preventing such a reality lay in the education system. If the Socialists in the United States took control of the education, then, they would have fertile ground to push their propaganda on young malleable minds.

João said that his instructors told him, "We must infiltrate science, technology, the military, politicians, law enforcement, the media, and intelligence services. In short, we must infiltrate all facets of production to control all that is the government.

"It becomes necessary to attract clever specialists and influential people to work with us. Without them, it is impossible to protect our interests. So, we create an atmosphere of friendly cooperation and conditions that will not allow them to break away. They must never have the slightest idea of what is happening under the surface of prying eyes. When our goals are achieved, they will be removed entirely from any influential position."

Then he introduced a new subject. A phrase associated with Lenin, "useful idiots." "This group's function is essential," he said. "They specialized in gossip. Everyone knows that the gossiper avoids the liar label; it is the denier that is the liar in the eyes of the public.

"They approve selected words, phrases blessed as excellent, and other terms and phrases deemed terrible. The innocent is forced to use the approved words and phrases. Otherwise, one is labeled a traitor, racist, misogynist, or worse."

So how is this goal achieved?

João said by "repetitive diction, creating an echo chamber, asking rhetorical questions, and repeating the problems in the answers, the selection of stereotyped adjectives and the dismissal of an attitude or fact by the simple expedience of approving and disapproving words and phrases reduces the people's freedom of expression and forces them to be indoctrinated into our beliefs or suffer the consequences."

Chapter

8

The approach to Wake Island was rough. For the last couple of hours, the weather had gradually deteriorated with swirling winds, intermittent rain, and decreased visibility, having all the ingredients for a dangerous landing.

All the while, the Clipper's fuel reserves were slowly draining to dangerous levels. Along our route, we encountered strong headwinds and spent more precious fuel than planned. We had to land the aircraft; there was no other alternative.

In the meantime, the anxiety level was palpable with every single passenger, including me, and I was a pilot. I could just imagine how the other less experienced passengers must have felt as we made our rocky approach to a landing. Most everyone had a white-knuckle grip on the handles of their seats. Many just closed their eyes and looked up. Others prayed.

The pilots approached the landing carefully, but in the same way as any other water landing. They leveled off just above the water surface, increased power sufficiently to maintain a rather flat attitude until conditions appeared more acceptable, and then reduced power to touch down. Then, rough bouncing occurred, and power was increased just enough to keep the craft under control above the wave tops. As if heaven offered safe passage, calmer waters appeared just in time to bring the seaplane down safely but far beyond the normal landing area. It took a little longer to taxi to the terminal, but we were safe and sound. Finally, we disembarked, a bit anxious, and glad to be on terra firma.

The rough landing damaged three propeller blades. The meteorologists forecasted strong winds for the next twenty-four to thirty-six hours. It would take at least that much time to repair or replace the damaged propellers. Everyone was happy to be on dry land, and we took advantage of the opportunity by exploring the island.

I was sitting on a log, appreciating the beauty of the restless ocean. Wave after wave rolled to the shore, creating a sound that relaxed my most inner being. Above me was a flight of albatross, affectionately called "gooney birds." Like a squadron of military aircraft preparing for landing, they identified wind direction. Heading into the wind, they control the rate of descent, decreasing speed as they gracefully make their landing. Then, they hit the ground with the grace of a Charlie Chaplin skit. Some tumble over mounds of sand, and, after rolling a couple of times, stand upright and shake the sand off their bodies as if nothing had happened. Others let down their landing gear at the last instant and run on the sand for a little bit before tripping over and falling face-first on the beach. It was a fantastic sight, entertaining, and at the same time, a great lesson. We all could be riding a streak of good fortune, and just as quickly, stumble into ruin. The lesson—getting up, like these magnificent birds, shaking the dust off of one's body, and moving forward.

I saw a man walking blunderingly towards me like a gooney bird. It was João. Interesting how a man of sophistication walked so awkwardly. He was a gooney bird. He was graceful in flight and awkward on land.

We wondered how long it would be before our journey would continue, if the weather was about to improve and how the propeller repairs or replacement were progressing. Then, João got that look again, as if he wanted to unburden his soul from sullied actions. Still, I felt like his confessor as he poured his heart out to me.

Never, ever criticize the Party's decision.

João told a story of a meeting. The gathering was set to critique a document. "A gentleman entered and made his apologies for being late and for not having had the time to read the material in question. The head of the meeting said 'not to worry, we have not seen or read the document either.' Then, he looked to the audience and continued, 'Nor have the majority of the delegates present here.'

"They condemned the document without reading it. I looked at the gentleman that arrived late, and he looked at me and shrugged his shoulders in disbelief. Although we knew that party decisions were sacrosanct, members do not violate party decisions, I was still struck by the utter incapacity to be fair.

"Critical thinking was not allowed. The party demanded blind obedience." He said, "Once self-denial is approved, the mind, instead of operating freely, becomes the servant of a higher and unquestioned purpose. To deny the truth is an act of service."

João stepped back, looking fearful as if he had seen a rabid dog. He said, "I was alone in arguing against the majority opinion when I made another sad discovery. Even those who agreed with me did not support me.

"Membership in Socialism meant defending the indefensible and dominating your fellow citizens to satisfy a very narrow self-interest. Instead of persuading reasonable men, they insult the assembly. I found myself covered in filthy ideas; I needed a way out of this false life that I had chosen." João looked exhausted as he looked out toward the horizon.

After João's talk, I thought that freedom of speech was Socialism's enemy. It was only their version of freedom of expression that had significance. A standard error of human thinking is to insist that a rule be universally applicable. Instead, it was the manipulation of freedom of speech that Socialists owned. They made their own rules as circumstances deem necessary. As far as I was concerned, Socialists have no moral code.

I thought: The struggle between secularism and believers in the afterlife has been around since practically the beginning of time. Marcus Tullius Cicero wrote: "For I am not one of those modern philosophers who maintain that our souls perish with our bodies and that death ends all."

I believe the heart of our culture is Christianity, the main reason the West is so powerful and how most classical literature has always been to teach morality. The Christian moral foundation of social and cultural life was what made possible the emergence of self-regulating markets, stressing individual rights, and the successful transition to Democratic politics.

Christianity, then, is the fiercest foe Socialism faces. The Socialist's dichotomy ignores the contributions of Christianity. That must be the reason they preach secularism with so much energy. The government then replaces God. Evil, selfish men take the place of a loving God. Overturn the altars; break down the temples; down with the gods!

I told João: "Men who claim to protect the people's rights, when in the seat of power, often forget their claims and become the deadliest of oppressors. So, it is imperative to observe the conduct of those in control with a free, unbiased press. Unfortunately, it is becoming more and more challenging to trust, to believe our journalists."

João replied: "If in America, any or all of what I just told makes it presence, it means that the media has chosen sides." The lapping waves never ceased attacking the shore as I thought about João's comment.

I thought that there is no perfect adaptation of man to society, yet Socialists try to put everyone in the same social box. Even though humanity is complex and not just one piece of the same pie. Every attempt to simplify this truth, every effort to reduce everything and everyone to the same common denominator is, and always be, sinister and dangerous.

João said that "Socialism is the belief that all of society can be altered by turning people into community-altering machines. Socialists take advantage of man's suffering by preaching that pain is the road to salvation.

He continued by saying "that the Socialist definition of man is that he was born, he suffered, and he died."

I thought of a more optimistic definition. "Man is born, grows to manhood, marries, produces children, works for his daily bread, dies, and his soul goes to a peaceful rest in the afterlife."

I cannot agree with the Socialist classification of man. I had witnessed friends and family members succeed and fail. "Reality is that other men with no more advantage than the next succeeded, and others with much more fail. Some people are weak, and others are strong. The physical and emotional needs of one are not the same as others. Some are beautiful, while others are ugly. Those with more celebrated talents and work ethics will receive greater rewards.

"Some people are born into families that provide all the opportunities for success, and yet they fail, while others born into dysfunctional families prosper. The unsuccessful will always envy the successful. There are no two people alike. The bottom line is that we are human beings with feelings and are not precisely the malleable machines that Socialism attempts to produce."

Chapter

9

The pre-flight checklist was completed with all systems green. We were about to embark on the next leg of our journey, Guam. Line handlers cast off the flying boat from the pier, and we made our way to our take-off position.

Flying smoothly at 10,000 feet without a cloud in the sky, I saw the point on the horizon where the sky and the ocean meet. It seemed so far away, yet it gave me a feeling of safety. I could see what was in front of me to avoid danger—that same horizon where the sky and the ocean meet is also present when overcast. Of course, we cannot see it, which made me think of the unseen perils that may be waiting for us during our routine lives. It is what lies beneath, the hidden, the undetected that worries me. It made me think of the long-lasting struggle between good and evil that started when Lucifer rejected God's laws.

Jealousy and the search for power made him attempt the overthrow of the almighty: the first attempted coup d'état! I decided that I had to see everything but believed little that people in power said. I thought, why is it that lies persist and become fact over time?

After all the time we had spent together, João and I were becoming friends. I found his conversation quite enriching. I felt sad for him even though I could not confidently pinpoint the source of his sorrow. However, in the back of my mind I kept wondering if he was trying to recruit me.

So, João went on: "People often fail to recognize malicious fraud—one thing is artificial, and another is real. When this type of fraud is successful, people classify it as smart and even crafty when, in reality, it is wickedness. The Socialist idea of playing the political game is not the same as yours and mine. They play to win no matter who or what they need to destroy to achieve their goal."

He described how the instructors in Moscow told them that the factories in the United States were dark, dirty, and either too cold or too hot, that the air was musty, that workers were forced to work long days that owners care little for their health and happiness, and that profit was what mattered the most.

He believed every word the instructors had told him until he arrived in New York and saw for himself the truth. João said: "I saw it with my eyes and heard it with my ears. That the American people frequently say that even the most mediocre person believed deep down that he can become the next millionaire or even president.

"During a visit to a factory in New York, cleanliness stood out. They did not look like our dark and dirty factories. All employees are correctly and tastefully attired. Once in the street, you cannot tell the difference between employee and employer. They wear the same outfits and behave in the same easygoing manner. There is no class warfare, as said by instructors in Moscow.

"Why should an employee be intimidated or hostile to his employer? They genuinely believe that someday they can be the boss. The only reason they are not the boss now is that the employer, at the moment, had better luck."

This thought made me reflect on the high power of "chance," which propels one either toward success or adversity. I felt that João must have felt like Jonah inside the belly of the whale as he resided in the dark belly of Socialism. Now in the United States, he saw the light. Under Socialism, the outside world was black and white—misery! Capitalism provided for a multicolored world—joy!

The proud merely wished to be left alone. The majority looked upon the well-to-do as people to be exploited. They knew what to say to get the advantages. João looked up to the sky as if communicating with a higher authority. He said, "All left-wingers in highly industrialized countries are nothing less than a farce. It is true because they make it their goal to fight against something that they do not want to risk destroying. They do not want to kill the golden goose that pays for all their unrealistic social projects."

João said, "Socialists lied and never knew that they had lied. When someone points out to them the untruth, then, they say that lies are beautiful. The same thing happens to history under Socialism. Year-by-year, sometimes month-by-month, *Pravda* corrected itself and rewrote editions of the official history books. The *Pravda* editors censored even Lenin, Marx, while historic monuments come tumbling down."

See, the creation of a secular state is a favorite idea of the radical intellectuals and the Socialists. In the meantime, the opportunists bide their time. The real policy of the Left is to abolish everything the Right had put forward.

Socialism abhors the Christian teaching of goodwill. The Left attacks Christianity's tenets. They devalued the sanctity of life, the importance of work, the formation of the family, and the centrality of faith. A Socialist civilization is one that believes that the State is the supreme being.

A man content with life, a man comfortable with his situation, a man who has enough money for his needs is not one ready for Socialist recruitment. Ironically, Socialists speak contemptuously of money, but seek it at every opportunity.

Socialism stifles the spirit of the individual. It hinders the opportunity for independent men to go up the ladder of financial independence.

Capitalism encourages risk-taking. The small business owner hires a new man and helps him grow out of poverty while bracing the man's self-confidence. Capitalism opens the way to success for all people willing to work. No person is worthier and more trusted than those who started at the bottom and left poverty behind by their hard work.

Socialism replaces the will to work. Some people may find that satisfactorily enough. They are willing to sign up for a government handout, but the vast majority of people would rather have the liberty to succeed or fail on their own.

With redistribution of wealth, what the government is really doing is promoting poverty and discouraging wealth. Then one has created the foundation for strife in society.

Simply, class warfare destroys cohesion and encourages hate and jealousy. It is just the type of environment to promote division among the population.

Nature got it right. Politicians got it wrong. The people's duty is better done when unhindered by roadblocks, rules, and regulations. The best way to help everyone is to allow people to help themselves as nature intended.

A politician's handout is designed to help the politician and only the politician. With their perceived benevolence, they are buying votes from those that would rather have the government help than go out to work. In other words, they prefer government dependency than the freedom to choose their way.

The government cannot guarantee happiness. No system can ensure satisfaction. The best we can do is to pursue happiness individually. Some find joy, even if only for a short while. Others never find happiness. Perhaps the best way to find happiness is to look inward and not outward. Life is not fair. The more government control, the less freedom the people have.

João thought that they were fighting for Spain's better future, that there was another pattern, perfect and beautiful. Instead, Socialism brought despair; there was no way out; a man was made to suffer. He wondered why so many people did things that were contrary to all their theories of life.

To the Socialist, life is a struggle, and the ethical rule that was suggested seemed to fit in with his predispositions. Of all virtues, justice is the most important. The weakest are protected from injustice, and the strongest are open to the same unbiased treatment as the lowest in society. Everyone, then, is held to the same standard, from the powerful to the lowliest citizen. We are all seeking a fair justice system; otherwise, there is no justice! When there is no justice, laws are invented that protect the powerful. Therefore, legislation must be cultivated and maintained, like a gardener protects and nurtures his plants and trees.

It is essential to guard against men of the empty show. These men are recognizable by their dissembling speech and countenance. They are only seeking their glory and remove justice from the country's equation. True justice takes root and grows as an elm tree as it spreads its strong branches protecting all. But those that seek personal glory through the pretense that cannot endure will water the tree of justice with poison.

Chapter

10

Following the 1898 Spanish-American War, Madrid ceded the small island of Guam to the United States of America. In December 1941, the Japanese took the island.

Guam, the tiny Pan American Clipper stop 1,500 miles east of Manila, was ill-prepared for war. The total fatalities of the Japanese invasion: seventeen Americans and one Japanese. It was going to take a much grander effort for the American forces to retake the island. For now, let us get back to my grandfather's story.

We had recently arrived in Guam, the penultimate leg of my trip. The flight to Guam had been smooth as if we were floating on a comfortable bed. After a quick nap and a refreshing shower, I met João for dinner. We had a beautiful view from the dining room. The lush vegetation of a tropical island was making our dinner conversation even more enjoyable.

It was during dinner that João finally told me that he was on the run. Up to then, I was not sure what was going on with his life. I now knew that he was not trying to recruit me. It was relief. He had broken with Communism, and his life was in peril. He knew too much, and the Communists' reach was long when they looked to make an apostate pay for his sins.

For João, a Spanish patriot, the straw that broke the camel's back was the internecine battle between the Communists, the Socialists, the unions, and the Anarchists in Barcelona.

He related how it all started when "the Communists ordered the surrender of all private weapons and the build-up of an armed 'non-political' police force that excluded trade union members. The Anarchists knew that if they surrendered their arms, the political power in Catalonia would keep theirs. Surrendering their weapons meant surrendering their lives."

"The government then started taking over strategic spots like the Telephone Exchange. Rumors began flying that the worker's building was being attacked. With that, armed Anarchists appeared on the streets, fighting broke out, and all work silenced.

"The Loyalists now fought amongst themselves while simultaneously challenging the Franco forces. The question everyone asked was: Is that an attempted Anarchist coup d'état, or was it a Socialist coup d'état? Someone had to be blamed for the internecine fight in Barcelona. The outcome was that the Communist-controlled papers blamed disloyal Anarchists and Trotskyists and accused them of stabbing the Spanish government in the back.

"It was well-known that since the beginning of the Spanish Civil War, the Spanish Communist Party grew by leaps and bounds and owned most of the political power as well as the propaganda machine.

"The Communist press blamed the Barcelona internecine war on the Marxist far-left worker's party, which was anti-Stalinist. The entire event was falsely represented not as a spontaneous outbreak, but a deliberately planned insurrection against the lawful government.

"Additionally, the Fascists received a piece of the blame. Franco and his people were shrewd enough to start a second civil war in the rear, thus paralyzing the government. This comedy was too much for me. How can you keep the deception forever? I asked myself, 'What am I fighting for?' The answer, not this falsehood, so I decided to move away from the Communist Party. I renounced the Communist Party and instantly became a traitor."

Then João gave me another piece of advice. He said, "Anyone who has studied Communist tactics knows that when dealing with political opponents, trumped-up charges is the norm. I came to the realization that workshopping Socialism from afar was one thing; however, living it was a completely different matter. I knew too much. My name was added to the liquidation list."

Retaking Guam from the Japanese took brutal fighting. The Battle of Guam lasted from 21 July 1944 to 10 August 1944. About 3,000 Americans died in combat while the Japanese Imperial Army suffered nearly 18,000 combat deaths.

Chapter

11

João continued his harrowing story. "Most of Barcelona's government buildings were riddled with bullet holes. For days, I moved constantly. I never slept in the same place two nights in a row for fear of the midnight knock on the door that meant my end. One day, I walked by the ruins of a church. It had been gutted during the fighting. There were piles of rubble everywhere, which made for an excellent hiding place where I could rest in relative peace. I made it my temporary home.

"The Communists even persecuted their most faithful supporters—the members of the International Brigade. When these foreign fighters attempted to return to their homeland, they were singled out as traitors. Many were picked up on false charges at the border and returned to jails in Valencia. Everyone was under suspicion."

He then told me that it was around this time that João ran into the two recruits he had co-opted during his university time in England. Both young men looked old and tired. The shabby clothes they wore hung loosely on their emaciated bodies. They had joined the International Brigades and had fought well against Franco's forces. Disillusioned with Communist tactics, they were on the run, trying to get out of Spain, just like João. They decided it was best to part ways in an attempt to get back to England and to safety. We parted ways wishing each other the best of luck.

João told me that when he became a Communist, he also became an atheist. He stopped believing in Christianity. Now that his life was in peril, he prayed. "Oh God, let me live until tomorrow." He said it over and over again. "Lord have mercy on me." He said that he begged for forgiveness, and rediscovered religion!

He continued his story, "In the days and weeks following the revolt, Barcelona's air felt heavy with evil with feelings of suspicion, fear, uncertainty, and hatred. The Communists were now securely in power. Everywhere you went, people spoke in whispers, as if the person next to you having a cup of coffee was a government informant.

"The jails were still full of prisoners left over from the revolt. Squalid prisons ripe for disease. The prisoners penned together in small rooms, like sardines in a can. There was little or no room to lie down, and they were always kept in the darkest and dampest places. The food was miserable. Prisoners were fed a filthy and insufficient diet of soup and bread. Anarchists and union members started to disappear in ones and twos overnight never to seen or heard from again. It was a nightmare of a situation.

"After many days of staying ahead of my pursuers, changing my appearance, and getting an occasional morsel of food to keep my strength up, I made my escape out of the Aragon province and finally out of Spain. I was able to take the forged identity of a fallen British citizen. Then, I fell in with a crowd of repatriated foreigners. This is when I found out my two recruits were captured and immediately shot by the Communists."

João said that he never spoke Spanish during his escape. Instead, he pretended to be an Englishman from Birmingham returning home. Thank God he spoke the language with a British accent. His studies at an English university were his savior. They finally crossed the border and entered France. He felt as if he had been born again. The air felt like freedom. At last, he left his Communist nightmare in the past.

The French authorities allowed him to enter their country, and he made his way to Paris, where he had friends who helped him finalize his escape. With a new identity, money, and an Argentine passport, he took a steamer to New York from the port of Le Havre.

I was at the edge of my seat and probably not even breathing as João told me about his escape from Spain. This man had been to hell and back. I told him he should write a book about his adventurous courtship with Communism and Socialism.

He said that he would think about, but for now he just wanted to get as far away from Spain as possible.

Chapter

12

At last, I arrived in Manila after a long, tortuous, yet enlightening trip. The Spanish Empire first set foot on the Philippine Islands in the sixteenth century. Manila, the capital, was founded on 24 June 1571. Following Madrid's defeat at the hands of the Americans in 1898, the islands became a charge of the United States of America. After forty-two years of American influence and centuries under Spanish rule, Manila was no longer Asian, yet not Western either. It was Manila, original Manila, majestic in its own way!

The "Pearl of Asia," as Manila was known, was nearly destroyed during World War II. In 1945, Japanese General Yamashita pulled his army from the capital and declared Manila an "open city." He hoped to spare the city from the fighting, much like Paris had been saved in 1944. What Yamashita did not know was that his orders were not strictly followed. Admiral Sanji Iwabushi and 20,000 Japanese marines were prepared to fight to the last man.

Manila, the very city in which MacArthur had spent so many years of his life, was a town where he was revered. In so many ways, the city that he had attacked and destroyed was his hometown. He would pass miles of rubble streets. He would see thousands of displaced families now camped on sidewalks. The beautiful Chinese, American, Spanish, and indigenous architectural structures were now gone along with thousands of Philippine lives.

I heard about General MacArthur's personality from several people, the briefing I had in Washington, DC, people I met who knew about him, and, finally, by reading everything in print that I could find.

The superlatives about the general were awe-inspiring: dedicated, charming, courteous, brilliant, and fearless. Other characteristics instilled caution and a bit of fear: arrogant, abrasive, imperious, and flamboyant.

I prepared as best I could to deliver the message I had brought from Washington. I was in my late twenties, physically fit, confident in my abilities, and I was not going to show fear. I believed that it would be a big mistake to do so. Besides, all I had to do was hand him the envelope that carried the letter, let him read it, and then wait for his response, which I would take back to Washington.

The appointment with the general was set; I would be the first of the day. He had just finished his Spartan breakfast of toast with butter and coffee. I was dressed in my best Brooks Brothers suit, which I had professionally pressed in the hotel. My shoes shone so that one could see his reflection. A crisp white shirt and a red tie completed the ensemble. I waited in the anteroom of his office and collected my thoughts. I had been briefed that his headquarters staff revered him. To them, he appeared courageous, unostentatious, and even warm. I had also been informed that he possessed superior intelligence. He was ready to receive me. I stood up straight and walked behind one of his staff officers. He introduced me to the general. Immediately, I felt the presence of a great man. The general instructed me to sit and asked if I wanted something to drink or eat. I said, "No, thank you, Sir," I recently had breakfast.

We got down to business. I stood up and handed him the envelope. He broke the seal and opened it and read the letter. It was one page, as best I could tell from my vantage point. He did not make a sound. He looked at me and thanked me for coming all the way from Washington. I was politely dismissed. That was the last I saw of the general. I did not have a message to bring back with me to the States. I had several days free to roam Manila and meet up with João before returning to the United States.

As I delivered the letter to General MacArthur, secretly, a much more important representative of President Roosevelt than I, on the other side of the world, was getting ready to meet with leaders of the United Kingdom.

In July 1940, President Roosevelt's emissary boarded a Pan American Clipper in New York. The Clipper was bound for Lisbon with a final London destination. Roosevelt's representative was a national hero. He had earned the Medal of Honor in World War I. His name: William J. Donovan. He was on his way to London to meet with the leadership of the British Secret Intelligence Service (SIS), the colorful Colonel Stewart Menzies. The Battle of France was over; France had surrendered to the Germans. The Battle of England was four days old.

About a month later, in August 1940, Donovan returned to New York on a British flying boat. In the ensuing months, he went back to Europe and witnessed the fighting in much of the Mediterranean. He flew thousands of miles, visiting one battlefield after another. He witnessed war again. He saw how terrible it was; how men died, cities were destroyed, and freedom was threatened. He returned to the United States and reported his findings to President Roosevelt.

The first step in establishing an American intelligence service happened on 18 June 1941, when Roosevelt approved the creation of the Office of Coordinator of Information (COI), with Donovan as director. Finally, on 13 June 1942, the Office of Strategic Service (OSS) was founded under Donovan's leadership. It was not long after that date that I became a member of the OSS. I left behind my barrister career and learned code, sabotage, and how to become invisible in plain sight. I fought the Germans in their own backyard. After the war, I was assigned to Berlin, a city that was divided into British, French, Russian, and American sectors. I would spend the rest of my life fighting Communism. After 1947, I fought as a member of the Central Intelligence Agency (CIA).

Chapter

13

Before João continued his journey to Hong Kong, where he hoped to start a new life, we had a few days of leisure and talked some more about the future. João had enough money to start a business or to invest in the Stock Exchange of Hong Kong (SEHK), the city's prosperous stock market. In the back of his mind, he had a dark foreboding feeling that he was being hunted down and one day would be assassinated.

João became a successful financier in Hong Kong. He started by investing in the SEHK for his benefit. As his success for buying and selling stocks grew, the word got around with other investors. He was encouraged to start his own investment business. Before long, he had a growing clientele. He was a fiduciary investor; he was smart and honest.

He met a wonderful Chinese lady, married her, and about a year later, the couple had a son. After a rough start to life, João was finding a silver lining of happiness. I was happy for him. We exchanged correspondence often. My job took me to different parts of the world, and sometimes, I was in Hong Kong, which was an excellent opportunity to visit him and his new family. His travels occasionally took him to Washington, DC, where we had the chance to reminisce about old times and discuss future events.

On one of those occasions when he was on a business trip to Washington, he asked me, "What were you really doing in Manila in 1940?"

I told him that I was delivering a letter to General Mac-Arthur. That my cover story was that of a government contractor surveying a building to purchase for the local American diplomatic staff.

He laughed out loud and said, "I knew all along that there was so much more to your travel to Manila than to purchase a building. The local embassy staff could have done that much more cheaply and quickly than sending a surveyor all the way from Washington, DC.

He looked me over with those trained eyes of a spy. Then, as if reminiscing, he gave a "huh," and we went back to our dinner.

Shortly after the first shots of the Korean War were fired, I read a blurb of a news story from the *Hong Kong Sunday Herald* that chilled me to the bone. "The body of João Sotelo was discovered yesterday morning by the Fung Wong Kai Stream. Mr. Sotelo was the owner of the Sotelo Investments, a firm registered with the Stock Exchange of Hong Kong. A single bullet to the back of the head from a .22 Caliber pistol caused immediate death. There was no exit wound. The small-caliber bullet ricocheted inside the skull, making mush of João's brain before stopping next to what was the cerebellum. Mr. Sotelo is survived by his wife and a young son.

PART
2

Chapter

14

While I was a student, I became more and more interested in history. In 2008, I earned my PhD in American History. In my mind, I often heard João's words, "Socialists are in it for the long game." These words made me think of the what-if scenarios.

I thought about what João said regarding the relationship between left-leaning politicians and left-leaning agents of influence. I thought of pilot fish. Pilot fish gather around sharks and feast on the shark's leftovers. Sharks do not eat pilot fish. The two of them have a symbiotic relationship. The pilot fish gains protection from predators, while the shark gains freedom from parasites.

The human species also has a kind of pilot fish—the journalist. This species looks for opportunities to please its master, the politician. The politician is an affable sort of man or woman. He or she makes himself or herself likable, and eventually, he or she wins people's trust.

He or she ingratiates himself or herself by being downright agreeable and complimentary. Even when you have doubts about his or her intentions, you let him or her into your circle of trust. When instead, you should be asking yourself, "Is something wrong?" But it feels good to be admired, to be liked. So, you ride the wave until it is too late to get off its deceitful crest, and you are slammed onto the rocky shores that break every bone in your body.

All things evil must start from innocence. The journalist repeats the politician's promises—promises that are impossible to keep. Everyone will have free health care, a job, a home, and happiness. People ready to be had buy into the propaganda all too easily. It is so easy to lie so effectively. People just want to believe.

The politician now makes his entrance onto the scene. He appears precisely as the journalist described him: generous, thoughtful, caring for everyone's well-being. What a man! What a woman! Soon, the media repeat his or her message until it becomes fact. Now in power, he will never let it go. All because a journalist prepared the battlefield for the politician's crowning.

The opposing political parties viewed the daily human struggle for an improved way of life from two different camps. One party believed in self-reliance that encourages people to choose their path to happiness. There were no limits. You could go as far as your hard work and intelligence could take you. There were failures, of course, but the people had the opportunity to choose their path—their path to self-actualization.

The other party had the edge when it came to an understanding of human weakness. They know that if you tell people often enough times that they must do this or that thing, they'll do it, and not ask why.

I thought about how some political philosophies never change. They just take a different name—Progressive!

Socialism in all prosperous, modern high-technology countries is really a sham. They make it their business to fight against something that they do not want to destroy. The Socialists in the United States cannot survive and thrive without Capitalism. Who is going to pay for all their giveaways without the productive, the innovative, and the risk-takers: the Capitalists!

Chapter
15

I'm on my way to Manila, Philippines, comfortably reclining in my business-class seat while smoothly flying at 37,000 feet. It was a Boeing 787 Dreamliner, a descendent of the Boeing B-314 flying boat. Two GEnx-1B/Trent 1000 engines power the modern aircraft at a cruising speed of 561 miles per hour, just a tad below the speed of sound (Mach 0.85) as we head west. What a contrast in travel from my grandfather's day, when his flying boat trekked above the Pacific Ocean at something less than two hundred miles per hour.

I was going to Manila for a history symposium hosted by the University of Santo Tomas, which, during the Japanese occupation, had been turned into a prison camp holding about 4,000 American and Allied civilians. I thought about my grandfather's conversation with João, how João fled from Communism, and was eventually murdered by that ruthless and unforgiving system.

The nonstop flight from San Francisco takes 16 hours and 44 minutes. The aircraft took a great circle route, which is the shortest distance between two points on the surface of a sphere, the earth. Map projections distort these routes confusing passengers; however, the great circle route is the shortest path between two locations. It is the reason why airlines fly these routes because they save time, fuel, and money. It is lightning fast when compared to my grandfather's flight from San Francisco to Manila in 1940. There was no need for island hoping to take-on fuel, supplies, and crew rest.

My grandfather passed away in 1999 at the age of 88. He experienced the Great Depression, World War II, the Korean War, the Vietnam War, and the Iraq War. He loved the United States of America and worried that our great nation might slide into the abyss of Socialist mediocrity or worse. He saw a mountain of destructive issues facing our country, most of the problems originating from within. The same Socialist problems he had witnessed in the 1930s, 1940s, and beyond. He was worried that history was about to repeat itself.

I took a look at what was happening today in our country.

In recent years, what kept the United States of America moving forward, no doubt, has been the optimistic outlook of most of its population. A feeling that tomorrow will bring better opportunities for all. Some of that feeling has to do with the historic emotion of patriotism. The belief that the United States is the shining city on the hill, an exceptionally blessed country allowing for equal opportunity for all. However, for at least the last sixty years, the main objective of the "Intellectual Left" and their associates in the mainstream media is to remove this passion from the people. Should they succeed, expect our

Constitution to be replaced with a rigid set of rules to keep the elite power brokers as rulers of the nation.

I was looking for a flight attendant when I saw a colleague. We were friends, but politically on opposite sides. He was going to the same symposium that I was attending. I knew that we would be debating each other from two different points of view. What I did not realize was that the debate would start right then and there during our flight to Manila.

Francisco Castro, known to family and friends as Frank, and like me was a PhD in history. His grandfather, Pedro Castro, a philosophy professor from the Universidad de Salamanca, founded in 1134, and where the Spanish writer and philosopher, Miguel de Unamuno had once been rector, put down his books and picked up a rifle and went to fight against the Franco forces and on the side of the Spanish Loyalists.

When Pedro realized all was lost and that Franco had won the war, he made his way into France. Eventually he went to live and work in Northern California where he found allies sympathetic to his cause in the University of California Berkeley. It was not long before he was teaching. Professing his version of what happened in Spain during the civil war and advancing his Socialists ideas.

Like me, Frank was greatly influenced by his grandfather's ideas. Frank promoted Socialist ideals while I fought against them.

I often wondered if I would be allowed to promote my beliefs if Socialists were in power in the United States?

Chapter

16

It was not long before Frank and I were discussing the 2016 election while enjoying a couple of cocktails. I said that "the presidential election put the brakes on the surging tide of Socialism in our country."

As I described what transpired that day, I could see that Frank was preparing a rebuttal.

I said, "On election day, Tuesday, November 8, 2016, the American people went to the polls to elect their next president. The Democratic candidate went to vote in her upscale neighborhood in one of New Jersey's suburbs. She was confident that she would be the president-elect by the end of the day.

"That evening, news networks started reporting early results. By the late evening, it looked like the election was going to be a close one, which pundits had not expected. The early morning hours of 9 November indicated that the election was a horse race. Then, the Democratic candidate's campaign manager addressed the enthusiastic devotees who had gathered for a triumphant celebration at the Javits Center. Instead of celebrating, the campaign manager told the devasted crowd to go home. The group now knew that their candidate would not be the next president of the United States, and they cried."

What if the losing side would not accept the results of the election and was determined to remove the duly elected president? I thought of a series of what-if scenarios.

How about this one, Frank?

"A week after the election, a clandestine meeting takes place in the imposing and isolated home of a Globalist billionaire. They met in a futuristic room. A large screen dropped from the ceiling. The men put on their wireless earphones. The meeting was recorded. The room was enclosed by bulletproof, floor-to-ceiling windows that revealed a scenery framed with majestic snow-covered mountains. Bristlecone pine, blue spruce, Douglas fir, and lodgepole pine dotted the verdant landscape up to the tree line. It was an inspirational sight, a place to think and to plan.

"The gentleman was a well-known financier born in Eastern Europe. He understood that he need not stand at the center of the storm; instead, he merely floated at its circumference. He was prepared to initiate a quiet coup d'état from afar.

"Still quite energetic for his age, he had brilliant blue eyes close to the bridge of his nose, like a wolf, and thin crimson lips that seldom smiled. He felt that the world was inhabited by beings who are not one-tenth as smart as he. He often suspected as much, and it was decidedly unfair that he should not be the leader of a global organization. He had a great gift for organization, zero scruples, was resourceful and determined and lived for revenge.

"In 1956, when still an impressionable young man, he witnessed how Russian tanks supported by infantry rolled into Budapest, ending the inchoate Hungarian romance with democracy. He learned that ruthlessness was necessary, but so was skullduggery, betrayal, and blackmail. These were key tools to prepare the political battlefield.

"His wealth and power came with strings attached. He was also a little too deaf to anyone else's notion of policy. It was his way or..., you know the saying.

"The time was the mid-1960s; it was time to play the political game. He viewed people as a gambler sees his chips. The chips have an intrinsic value, and, in the game, there was no time for sentimentality—people were chips to be used as necessary and then discarded.

"You see, according to him, people are naturally depraved. They cannot see how willing they are to accept any initiative to benefit themselves no matter how immoral. It was okay to lie and to thieve. It was okay to herd people, like cattle to the slaughterhouse, and make them do his will.

"The way he took advantage of the masses to achieve his goal is so sad. It is as if the people are in a stormy sea, and their ship is about to flounder. Although there are plenty of life preservers to save them all, they don't recognize the lifeline to safety and perish with the ship.

"You take away the people's means of self-subsistence, family, and belief in a higher being. You lower their self-esteem until they become entirely dependent on the government for their survival. Simply, you take away anything that makes life worthwhile. There is a better way for them to live a better life, but they do not understand it. His mastery over helpless people is without comparison.

"A select group of powerful agents of influence from all walks of life, occupied the room. The cabal waited for the arrival of their overlord to begin the planning session.

"The goal was to turn the United States of America from a Capitalist to a Socialist nation. Then, the United States becomes "Global," like many billionaires and world leaders wanted to see the Earth governed."

I went on to describe my "what if" while Frank listened attentively. I was surprised that he did not cut me off while I spoke. Cutting people off in midsentence is one of the Socialist's favorite tactics. That and when the discussion is not going their way, they speak over what one is saying, that way the listener stops paying attention and the Socialist prevents the audience from hearing a different point of view that does not agree with theirs.

So, I continued without interruption. "The problem remained that men are limitless in creating despair, as the madman who tells himself that he knows what a person is capable of doing." Globalists discount different cultures, languages, cuisine, living standards. I looked intently into Frank's eyes and said, "Why is it that there is always a group of men that believe they have the best solution for governing the people? What or who gives them that right? Is it arrogance, or the will to power?

"Finally, the gentleman, let's call him the leader, spoke to the powerful gathering. He said, 'I am mad. I am mad because we should never have lost the election. We are this close'—he showed his thumb and forefinger about a millimeter apart—from taking over the United States. We had powerful people in government, media, industry, entertainment, and we still lost.'

"He went to say, 'The reason we lost was that we had an arrogant candidate. She did not work hard enough to win. She thought her name alone could win her the presidency. Her arrogance had no bounds. She called her opponents *deplorables* and other unflattering names. She should have known that one can only say such things after one has won.' He added, 'Now we must conduct damage control and protect our sources and methods.' Then he looked intently into each person in the room with his menacing blue eyes and said, 'You all have been provided with sealed envelopes with instruction. Chin up and create mayhem.'

"I saw the cabal organized like the Mafia and acted just as ruthless. Why not? The leadership pyramid and methods were proven. At the top was the boss with his trusted advisor. Then came the underboss, in this case, the men that now sat at the table. Below them came the proven officers that had an army of devotees under them: the wannabees who were ready to do anything for recognition. They were the type of people, hard people, soulless people, that could only see beauty if it was pointed out to them.

"No one got wind of the 'omnium gatherum,' a true testament to the alliance, professionalism, and training that united the conspirators. This cabal managed its business professionally."

"They now broke up into different groups with different responsibilities, but with the same goal of taking down the current president of the United States.

"The leader then added one more word of wisdom, 'now gentlemen, remember we are sharks and our pilot fish will do the hard and dirty work. Never forget that the American people are easy to deceive. There is not a moment to lose. Roll on!'

"There was a roar of laughter as the room emptied out."

Frank looked at me and took a swallow from his cocktail.

Chapter
17

Group A's responsibility was to promote the Duller report. For weeks in advance of the report's release, the mainstream media salivated with greed thinking the report would take down the president.

All the TV, radio, and online media pundits predicted that the president's days were numbered. Group A pushed the media hard to get every American into believing that the president had in fact colluded with the Russians to win the election. That the president was not the legitimate president of the United States of America. The legitimate president was waiting on the side lines for the coup d'état to succeed.

The mainstream media was in a state of joy as they waited for Mr. Duller to deliver his report to the public. Their house of cards came crumbling down one afternoon.

It happened as swiftly as Usain Bolt running the 100-meter dash. It was over, the president was exonerated, and the "Left" and its media allies were in total panic. The *Report on the Investigation into Russian Interference in the 2016 Presidential Election* could not find any collusion between the Russians, the president, and the president's team.

Group A had some quick work to do and basically discredited Duller, their hero. They said that it was a dull report—full of nonsense, half-truths, and innuendos. They said that they were not even sure that Duller had a hand in its writing.

They had to keep secret when the investigation began. The American people must never know if the investigation began before or after the president was elected. The American people must never know, on what evidence was the investigation started. And they must never know how many intelligence agencies were involved in the investigation. The American people must never find out the answers to these questions. Sources and methods must be protected.

However, the Group A was pleased that the former Intelligence Director had a trick or two up his sleeve. When asked questions by the "bipartisan" Congressional panel, the former director repeatedly said that the question was out of his purview or that he needed to refer to the report before answering. He played rope a dope with the panel.

Another result of the report that made Group A happy was that it created a precedent by which any Socialist politician could summon the people to create doubt in a future presidential election, unless, of course, they were the winners.

Now that the report was published, Group A knew that it was not the duly elected president, or his team, that committed any infractions leading up to the 2016 election. The abuses were committed by the Democrats and their allies in the Department of Justice, State Department, the FISA court, the FBI, the CIA, the DNI, and the Democrats in the House and Senate.

The best tactic in this case was to attack the president and his team despite being exonerated by the report. Group A's job, now, was to create more doubt regarding the presidency. The broadcasting of lies, half-truths, and innuendos against the president was front and center, but more important was the protection of the individuals in the different departments, agencies, and Congress.

Group A, secretly, admitted that the report was a complete failure for the Socialist and Globalist cause. They expected so much more. They hoped that the report's conclusion would provide clear evidence against the president, but that was not to be.

They knew that the report's unanswered questions were alarming. The Group had to prevent suspicion that US intelligence and law enforcement operators had spied on Americans. That the attacks were from within our government. It was not hostile action taken by foreign intelligence agencies or even terrorists. The people must never find out the truth. They must never ask: "What may happen in future elections if the conspirators go unpunished?"

Chapter

18

I told Frank that I understood why Democrats felt disheartened by their defeat in the 2016 election. They thought they had victory in the bag from the moment their candidate decided to run for president. Who could possibly defeat this well-known person, famous in some circles, despised in others, who had been running for president for most of her adult life?

The losing side, no matter how deserving they may think, does not have the right to disparage the rightfully elected president and attempt to remove him from office.

Thank God for the Electoral College, which our Founders had included into our Constitution.

The election was settled when the Republican nominee received the required number of votes from the Electoral College. This is the way the American people have selected their president since the first presidential election.

Of course, now, the Democrats and their allies want to do away with the equalizer that is the Electoral College. Without it, the country would be governed by the Socialist and Globalist voting block in many of the large states on both coasts of our country. The middle of the country would really be "fly over country" forgotten and punished.

I told Frank that "I was alarmed that the Socialists looked forward to the end of the Electoral College. That they, if they took power, they would have open borders, higher taxes, sixteen-years-old and felons voting in presidential elections, as well as increasing the number of judges sitting on the Supreme Court."

I said: "How do the average America people convince the Socialists that treason against the ballot-box is dangerous and that they are playing a desperate game that may cost many lives?

I went on to say that "Party lines have shriveled. Landmarks disappear before the eruption of untruthful attacks. Still, it is so tough to believe that the Democrat leadership and their allies and the mainstream media have raised their hand against the Constitution of our country when they have been fairly beaten."

Frank agreed that the changes proposed by Democrats are dangerous and could lead to one party government. He knew that someday the Democrats would take control of the presidency. The Constitution must remain as is for perpetuity.

Chapter

19

Frank and I engaged in another mini debate while flying just below the speed of sound and at 37,000 feet.

Frank, I said, "I think the Democrat Party is really the Socialist Party."

"Is it the Democrat goal to turn America Socialist? Are the Democrats really closet Globalists?"

I said, "What is happening in the United States today reminds me that the Ottomans called the city of Constantinople—the Red Apple. The Ottoman Empire were winning wars all over the Balkans, but Constantinople stood there as a reminder that Christianity lived and prospered in that walled city.

"For years the Ottoman's attacked Constantinople and each time failed to breach the walls. The city stood there defiantly before the Turks. The city held up until 1453, when a young and great Turkish leader by the name of Mehmed II and commonly known as Mehmed the Conqueror, finally defeated the inhabitants of the city.

"The city was besieged for weeks. The city became a little weaker each day as the defenders' injured mounted, food supplies dwindled, and the treasury reserves that paid for the armies defending the city were exhausted.

"Large modern Turkish cannons battered the city wall, but the city held out. As the defenders fought back, they prayed that Christian assistance would come from the west. They in fact received assistance from Giovanni Gustianni Longo, a Genovese soldier of fortune, but he and his highly trained men would not be enough to hold back the Turks. It was too little and too late.

"The Turks were becoming frustrated because despite their superior forces and modern cannons they could not take the city. Their dead and injured continued to grow with each passing day and morale among the troops started to turn ugly. Some in the Sultan's staff were dismayed by what the young leader was doing. They thought it was time to call for a truce and try to take the city sometime in the future.

"The Sultan would have none of that talk. He refused to give up.

"The siege turned in favor of the Turks when from within the walls of the city some in Emperor Constantine's staff commenced secretly working with the Turks. The betrayal by the emperor's closest advisors opened the gates for the Sultan to finally take over the city. Traitors from within helped take down the city.

"Many a Byzantine fled to the west from Constantinople. These Christians had a safe haven waiting for them in Italy, Spain, France, and other Christian nations in the west.

"The same cannot be said should the United States of America, the "Red Apple," be conquered by the Socialist and Globalists. Think about it, Frank, there would be nowhere else to go. Game, set, match over!"

Chapter

20

Group B now took the baton from Group A. Their responsibility was to make the governing of the country as difficult
as possible for the president and his party. To continue to throw
wrenches into the wheels of progress.

The Socialists were angry of their defeat. The honor of the
presidency went to the Republican candidate. The first really
American president in years. He was not a "Globalist." Even
previous Republican presidents were, at least a little bit, "Globalists." The president-elect repeatedly told those willing to
listen, that for him, it was always "America First." He was proud
and unashamed to put America first after so many years of
being relegated to the whims of the "Globalist" crowd.

Group B went to work.

They set their sights on the president. From that moment
on he would suffer the attacks of the mainstream media by day
and by night. Any other man would have folded like a lawn

chair after the vicious assaults that he and his family endured, but the slings and arrows made him even stronger. Of course, this made the Socialists even madder and also more frustrated.

This president was unlike other Republican presidents. This one fought back. This one returned fire. This one exposed the mainstream media for what it was—propaganda!

The Globalists do not surrender easily. They had an ace in the hole for use only in the direst situation. It was called an "insurance policy." Group B was about to execute its ace in the hole.

I kidded with Frank and asked him if he was part of the scheming club that had met out west behind closed doors in some secure location to overthrow the president?

He said I was crazy, but with a smile.

Group B went to work. They searched for an opening that would allow them to implement the "insurance policy."

One thing one can always say about the Globalists is that they are well trained and are determined to achieve their goal. "If at first you don't succeed then try, try, again."

The Group knew that the collusion with the Russians scheme did not work. There must be something else that they can pin on the president and take down his government, they thought.

The opportunity came about the summer of 2019. A conversation between the Ukrainian president and the American president takes place. Spies within the administration leak the conversation. At this point a "volunteer" is required to move the case forward before the public.

Someone with a debt to pay is ordered to be a whistle-blower. The Group knew exactly the right person for the job. This person has no recourse but to obey or his past mischiefs would be exposed for all to see.

The mainstream media takes over the duties of attacking the president around the clock. More lies, innuendos, and half-truths are sprinkled over the airwaves day and night. The Democratic leadership in the House of Representatives throws up a Hail Mary Pass—impeachment. Two articles are hastily drawn up: 1. Abuse of power. 2. Obstruction of Congress. A futile attempt at taking down the president, which also fails.

Group B failed in its attempt to take down the president, but they do not surrender.

Chapter

21

I said to Frank, "Where to begin to unravel this lie? How to expose the witch hunt when the mainstream media acts as the Socialists storm troopers making gaping holes for lies to walk through undisturbed while simultaneously providing top cover for Socialists propaganda? The Socialists blame everyone but themselves when their policies go awry, and, then, the mainstream media gives them cover and turn the table and put the blame on the evil Capitalists."

"So, tell me what you really think about the media," said Frank with a smirk on his face.

"Okay," I said.

"The way to begin unraveling this Socialist Gordian Knot against the president is to look back at what João told my grandfather in 1940. I compared the Communist tactics and strategy João discussed with my grandfather to the tactics and strategy employed by the Socialists today. It turns out that are incredibly similar.

"You see, Frank, Socialism is the fruit of the fusion between government and the classroom, the laboratory in which left-leaning politicians, educators, and bureaucrats, crazy scientists, formulate experiments in 'Globalism.' It is an idea easily traced to the Russian Revolution of 1917. A worker's paradise, global domination, the end of nationalism.

"Press reports alleged that the president associates had ties to Russian politicians. A specious 'dossier' was generated, and an espionage campaign hatched to tarnish him and his team's reputation and eventually remove him from office.

"The word *dossier* originated with the French secret police. It is a complete life record of an individual. Everything that seems likely to be of interest to the authorities: an all-encompassing report on relatives, anyone who appears to be going up the ladder of success, and any renown family connection. To the point, a 'dossier' is nothing more and nothing less than an espionage tool used by intelligence services against its own citizens.

"The behind-the-scenes collaborators of this unseemly act must never indulge a sense of fair play or hamper secret operations with ethics or moral baggage. They must stand ready to act as a criminal would, desperate, with even acts of violence put beyond the goal of an overshadowing act. Rather than listening to the truth, the mainstream media promotes propaganda and gossip—active measures, really, to protect their Socialist allies."

Group B had resources inside federal law enforcement agencies, and bureaus. They knew about the close relationship between two married colleagues that were being less than honest to their respective spouses. These two probably fall in the useful idiot category, although they thought they were cleverer than most people.

Group B then pushes forward propaganda that relies heavily on a succession of baseless rumors, cleverly devised to influence public opinion while simultaneously minimizing loyalties and patriotic aspirations. They enjoy repeating stories, even when their accuracy is questioned, for they are extravagant, dramatic, and controversial.

Seeing what was transpiring before my eyes day in and day out, I was convinced that most journalists are a breed of people I could not trust.

I felt that "the majority of today's journalists grow up on party affiliation—mostly Socialists believers. That makes it difficult, if not impossible, for them to be evenhanded. They often think only as party hacks and not as free men. On one side, they put the truth, and on the other, they put forth policy. Now, these journalists morphed into active political operatives.

"They simplify every sentence and hammer it to the people by repetition. Turn on the television, and the indoctrination starts. From one news coverage to another, the exact untruthful phrase is repeated by liberal pundits until it becomes accepted as truth. What they say is right and must shine brightly; what the opposition says is wrong and dull. The Socialist's message must be painted white as virgin snow. The Capitalist's message must be painted black as coal.

"This loyalty to a political party handcuffs the journalist's freedom as well as besmirches the profession. Ethics are dismissed since it appears to be a pleasure to mislead, to lie, to create fear where there is none. There are plenty of enforceable ethical rules; however, they purposely fail because disobedience from above may bring down punishment, so they lose the nerve to affirm the truth.

"Socialist ideals come first, individual thinking prohibited. Party allegiance is supreme, and the branch that breaks from the tree must wither and die. The party's guidance is sharply defined. Its talking points, tactics, and strategy are determined by the principle that the end justifies the means. Humans do not deliberate about purposes, but about the factors. The clever man proceeds to consider which choice will provide it most efficiently and best."

I took a breath before continuing my harangue. Good ole Frank listened, although, most probably, not believing a word I said.

I continued, "most of the evils that plague American journalists today are due to the lack of courage. It does not take courage to be a Socialist journalist, since a Socialist journalist, in their view, is obviously a smart upstanding citizen. If one fights the mainstream media, then, expect slings and horrible arrows launched in your direction. First, one is classified as ignorant. The name-calling does not cease, instead it gets personal. One is a racist, a homophobic, a misogynist, or even a white supremist. Anyway, the mainstream media is entirely biased; the majority of them act as a weapon for the political party they serve."

Socialist leaders trap people into believing in a better future, but they can only hold on to power by the sword. They confuse the language by dictating what can be said and what cannot be said. In this state, it does not matter whether you are good or bad, for, in this state, everyone is a loser. They rob the work of the creators of beauty and call their culture theft.

The Group knew that it was important for their journalists go outside the bounds of their responsibilities. One way is by becoming an actor more so than a journalist.

There were some journalists in particular that fit that mold perfectly. A high-powered news network that promoted Socialist ideals has such a "journalist." In fact, the Group knew that this journalist was their golden boy of news reporting. A journalist that enjoyed sparring with his political opponents, making himself the center of attention.

Only his antics make for primetime coverage. He is incapable of critical analysis; his commentary is totally partisan. He is simply a political activist and not a journalist in the traditional sense. But he did criticize everything the president and his administration did. Group B had their man.

Along these lines, it made me think about what João had told my grandfather so many years ago. I remembered what he said about money, ideology, compromise, and ego (MICE). I also remembered what my friend, Erica, had told me. She said that "most Cubans are conservatives. They despise Communism because they witnessed firsthand how that system destroyed their island."

With Erica's words in mind, I asked myself "Why is a journalist of Cuban heritage the face of a Socialist television network?"

Modern agents of influence are destroying freedom of the press from within. It is almost as if before they divulge any news, they meet in some secret place, real or virtual, and decide how to move forward. They are as a well-drilled and disciplined as a Marine Battalion Landing Team.

They are in step, never deviating a millimeter from approved talking points. They censor positive news, or they underreport them. For example: the excellent economy, lowest unemployment numbers for all people, the destruction of ISIS, protecting our borders, and bringing home our military from years of foreign wars. Instead, they highlight untruths and repeat the same untruth, half-truth, gossip, and innuendos throughout the day on the radio, TV, and internet.

The Socialists create lies, and the media distributes them.

Chapter

22

Group C came into action. This team was composed of quasi-scientists and failing meteorologists. But they could spin a yarn with the best recontours. Globalist absolutely loved the climate change movement.

The movement had started in the late1970s, but it never really took traction.

Group C's leader provided background to his team. "It was in the 1970s and before 'global warming' was invented, that 'global cooling' was the buzz phrase. Climate experts claimed that 'the earth was cooling quickly and there would be famine because crops could not grow in such cold conditions. Children in Ipanema Beach would be building snowmen instead of sandcastles.

"The *Boston Globe* ran the following headline in 1970: 'Scientists predict a new ice age by the 21st century.' The *Washington Post* published a Columbia University scientist's claim that the world could be 'as little as 50 or 60 years away from a disastrous new ice age.' Finally, not to be outdone, in 1978, the *New York Times* headline claimed a team of international scientists predict a 'cooling trend in the Northern Hemisphere.'"

The group's leaders said that when the cooling trend failed miserably to gain traction, a new tactic was needed.

"We found it when a different set of international scientists endorsed an Associated Press headline from 1989 that stated, 'Rising seas could obliterate nations: UN officials.' The article confidently reported that entire nations would be gone by the year 2000 if the world failed to reverse global warming."

It is difficult to promote a falsehood when the facts are against you.

"The Arctic Ocean is warming up, icebergs are growing scarcer, and in some places, the seals are finding the water too hot according to a report from the Commerce Department yesterday from the Consulate at Bergen, Norway.

"The reports from fishermen, seal hunters, and explorers all point to a radical change in climate conditions and hitherto unheard-of temperatures in the Arctic zone.

"Exploration expeditions report that scarcely any ice has been met as far north as 81 degrees and 29 minutes. Soundings to a depth of 3,100 meters showed that the gulf stream still very warm. Great masses of ice have been replaced by moraines of earth and stones, the report continued, while at many points well-known glaciers have entirely disappeared.

"Very few seals and no white fish are found in the eastern Arctic, while vast shoals of herring and smelts which have never ventured before so far north are being encountered in the old seal fishing grounds. Within a few years, it is predicted that due to the ice melt, the sea will rise and make most coast cities uninhabitable."

This article dates back to **November 2, 1922**, almost one hundred years ago. An Associated Press reporter wrote the article, and the *Washington Post* published it for all to read. Some things never change! Fossil fuels had nothing to do with a warmer than usual November in 1922. Most probably, it was just nature running its cyclical course.

The Globalists and their scientist allies claimed that the earth is heating up because of the use of fossil fuels. Perfect, they had identified a villain everyone can associate with; fossil fuels the source that we all depend on to enjoy a better way of life.

Why is it that the United States is always the culprit when it comes to climate change, when China, India, Malaysia, and Russia are the real culprits?

John Polkinghorne, a British theoretical scientist, theologian, writer, and Anglican priest, wrote in his book *The Polkinghorne Reader: Science, Faith, and the Search for Meaning* that "There is a popular account of the scientific enterprise which presents its method as surefire and its achievement as the inexorable establishment of certain truth." Science and observation can be wrong. Frequently it takes multiple experiments to get to the truth.

People need to acknowledge that personal beliefs play a role in scientific endeavors.

Chapter

23

Group C had a formidable challenge before them. Somehow, they had to keep people's attention glued to the man-made evil, to climate change. Luckily their bag of tricks was full of volunteers eagerly willing to promote their Globalist agenda.

The Group was completely aware that some leaders are becoming more arrogant, believing with complete certainty that the state exists to serve them and not the other way around. There is nothing new under the sun. There are, however, renamed successful propaganda schemes dedicated to deceiving the public. Some believe in man's conquest of nature.

Their dream of scientific planning will one day come true. They understand what man's power over nature means; it's really about the influence of some men over other men. It was, after all, about power!

Each generation has its own ideals. The old is discarded for new thinking. Power is exercised over its predecessor. A new picture is created. The Socialists are trying to do just that—achieve emancipation from tradition and gradual control of the natural process, even if they have to deceive all humankind, or at a minimum, the American people.

Between 66 BC and AD 500, the world was to end four times. Between AD 500 and 1000, that number grew to seven, and the number grew another seven times between AD 1000–1500. From 1500–2000, end of the world predictions grew to the unprecedented number of one hundred and twenty. Between 2000 and 2018, the naysayers predicted the end of the world twenty-eight times.

The media, in support of climate-change politics, warned of several impending disasters in the last fifty years. Famine, drought, an ice age, and even disappearing nations.

Jesus Christ said, regarding the end of the world, "But of that day and hour no one knows, not even the angels of heaven, but my Father only" (Matthew 24:36).

The most recent end of world prediction was announced in 2019 by the most prominent false prophet of them all: a twenty-nine-year-old politician from New York. A wise man said, "I do not expect old heads on young shoulders." Maybe she is another useful idiot. In any event, tune the antennas on your tinfoil hat if you decide to follow her lead.

Group C had their useful idiot. They could ride her idiocy as long as it was useful. When she became a burden, and it was only a matter time before she did, then, she would be discarded like a pair of old shoes.

According to the young politician, she said with certainty, that the world ends in 2031.

She awakes in the middle of the night from a nightmare smartly dressed. She records a video for YouTube. She tells us that she cannot sleep at night. Cities will soon be underwater, and she will not have children for fear that climate change will destroy the world as we know it today. The future is dark and fossil fuels are the culprit.

Nothing in nature is regular; however, there are exceptions. A solid average of uniformity, but not complete. But the mainstream media does not discourage her from promoting her bizarre prediction.

Some people seem to think that "matter" moves in an indeterminate fashion; the fact is that "matter" moves of its own accord. That is what real scientists tell us.

Socialists politicians reject Newton's orderly universe and accept Darwin's chaotic world. Darwin's world allows them to shift their political positions to fit their goals.

They also claim that science and especially climate scientists are infallible. The truth is that all possible knowledge depends on the validity of reasoning and not on "scientific" inferences. If humankind's argument is not valid, then, no science can be 100% correct.

When scientists profess to explain our reasoning without introducing an act of what is known, then all one has is a theory without argument. This comparison avoidance of just introducing inferences that agree with your ends are their goals. They offer what feigns a full account of nature's behavior. When on further inspection, there is zero room for the acts of knowing on which the value of thinking, as a mean for the truth. When facts get in the way, they reject them.

For those who believe in reason, and precisely the reason for God, God is older than nature. God created the world and, therefore, nature. I know there is no proof except for what is written in the Bible. This belief is called faith.

I know that scientists live for proof. For some scientists, it was the "Big Bang" that created nature, even though no one can really prove that either. But let's say it was the Big Bang that created the universe! Then, the question should be, who pressed the button that ignited the Big Bang?

To believe that God is a product of nature is absurd. Some do not understand that premise—or maybe they do, but the political lie is more important. Nature is not an object that can be presented either to the senses or the imagination. The most remote deductions can only reach nature.

What we imagine only exists for our awareness. However, some politicians, by the use of words, induce other people to build for themselves false pictures.

Group C needed an arrogant, self-serving, infallible modern-day agent of influence. He was the host of a Sunday morning political show. He was convinced that climate change science is correct. One Sunday morning before speaking to his regular aficionados, his lips are pressed together in controlled anger, and then he pushed out his lower lip. Now, as he is speaking, his lips narrow—a sure sign of anger. There is no discussion about the issue, and he will not debate any dissenters on this show that questions the validity of climate change science.

The kind of analysis one makes on any complex issue depends on the purpose of your point-of-view. In his case, the view is Globalism.

He talks down to people who do not accept climate change. Many like him even show their contempt for climate change skeptics by calling the names like "flat earthers." Now, name-calling is a sure way to create more enemies, but he does not care.

He rejects the findings of the Nongovernmental International Panel on Climate Change (NPICC). An international network of scientists first convened in 2003 that examined the same climate change data used by the IPCC and came to different conclusion.

I said the big mistake the show host makes is that "he fails to see his mistake by preventing debate. He makes up more and more elaborate theories that make no sense to the average person. The main point is that none of these complicated theories would be required, had he allowed for debate and for the people to decide."

The Group's fear lies with the NIPCC's 800-page report on scientific research that contradicts much of the IPCC's conclusions. Therefore, the need for rabid and angry supporter of the Globalist's climate change conclusions. Otherwise, there would be discussion that would put doubt on people's minds watching the program.

NIPCC's report sheds light on the subject and discusses the numerous deficiencies and shortcomings of the IPCC report. Issues that alter even the very sign (plus or minus, warming, and cooling) of earth's projected temperature response of rising CO_2 concentration.

Light would also be shed on more bad modeling by the ICC. The model-derived temperature sensitivity of the earth—especially for doubling of the preindustrial CO_2 level—is much too large, and feedback in the climate system reduces the sensitivity values that are an order of magnitude smaller than what the IPCC employs.

NIPCC's findings also point out the following: Real-world observations do not support the IPCC's claim that the current trends in climate and weather are unusual and, therefore, the product of CO_2-induced global warming. The IPCC also overlooks or downplays the many biological benefits to be accrued from the ongoing rise in the air's CO_2 content.

Furthermore, there is zero evidence that CO_2-induced increases in air temperature will cause exotic plant and animal extinctions, either on land or in the ocean.

Finally, there is no evidence that CO_2-induced global warming is, or will be, responsible for increases in the incidents of human diseases or the number of lives lost to extreme weather.

Chapter

24

The Founders based the foundation, the fundamental values of our Constitution on Isaac Newton's findings, the great English mathematician, physicist, astronomer, theologian, and author. Newton saw the order in the universe and, in particular, our solar system.

The four seasons: fall, winter, spring, and summer, follow a definite pattern. Gravity keeps the planets from bumping into each other. Nature has checks and balances. It is a clear and clean system that governs our universe, whether you believe that it was created by God or by the phenomena of the "Big Bang."

It is a system that it is always the same, you can depend on it, and it will always be there. Our founders found beauty in this order, and it became the blueprint for our Constitution. It provided the steps, the checks and balances that prevent one branch of the government from becoming too strong. Beauty happens!

Charles Darwin was an English naturalist, best known for his contribution to the science of evolution. Darwin's theories became the early Socialist's idea for governing. They saw government as a living organism. They viewed government under the theory of organic life.

The good and the worthless both desire glory, honor, and power. The good person works on the right path, while the worthless, having no honorable traits, compete, using betrayal and deception. And why is it that the bad want many more favors than the good?

Fundamental rights and liberties only exist in the mythological world, Socialists claimed. For Socialists, people follow laws because the consequences of obeying them are a whole lot better than the results of disobeying. Socialists would use the stick a lot more and the carrot a lot less.

Picture this 2020 Socialist Presidential Platform. Open borders. All drugs legalized. All forms of finance, including banking, insurance, stocks, bonds, mortgages, are under the control of the federal government. Felons, behind bars, allowed to vote. Private businesses and homeownership forbidden. All forms of transportation, mines, oilfields, solar farms, wind farms, hydroelectric plants, public utilities, communications, think tanks, and education—everything is nationalized. A presidential panel will be appointed to determine how the nation's production and wealth will be distributed to the people. Once the board reaches a decision on distribution, an individual or organization is forbidden to make unfair claims against the government.

Freedom of religion is guaranteed as long as people practice their beliefs inside their homes. No individual can earn more than $750,000 per year. Inheritance will be topped off at $2,000,000.

No individual or family can have a fortune of more than $5,000,000. Any monies above those sums go directly to the government's treasury.

This nightmare could happen. Socialists do not care whatsoever for liberty, inalienable rights of the individual, and the pursuit of happiness. All they care about is someone else's money and property. What they want is power. Nearly all their political ideas consider raids upon capital, even when feigning freedom from desiring riches.

Chapter

25

The Socialists and their Globalists allies have one ace in the hole that will continue to provide new recruits for years to come. That ace in the hole is the Teacher's Union. Don't you agree, Frank?

I said, "The secular Socialist education system emphasizes the primacy of the state over the individual in time and in moral authority. Patriotism and Judeo-Christian values are constantly attacked. Proven ethical and eternal truths principles are out!"

I said, "Man is nothing more than an organism that is molded by the environment, and the situation is continually changing, like in Darwin's ideas. Teaching children any of the absolute morals and ethics is a complete waste of time.

"Reading, writing, and arithmetic does not matter in their education system. Socialist indoctrination is ongoing, no matter the subject being taught. This will eventually lead to the complete destruction of individualism.

"Essays like *Self-Reliance* by Ralph Waldo Emerson are no longer taught at schools. Dependency on government handouts is much more valued than individual reliance. The result is that many students blindly follow the Socialist indoctrination never knowing of a better path in life. People do not realize until it is too late that they are being controlled by the oppressive government.

"Once this goal is accomplished, the children willfully conform or adjust to the society they live in without giving it a second thought. In time, they will become adults and good citizens according to the Socialist ideology."

Frank response was simple but true, "The Teacher's Union is extremely powerful, and it will be difficult to break them up."

I thought to myself, "The political fight shaping up between Capitalism and Socialism made me realize that my grandfather's fears were real. Socialism is like the living dead—zombies. The dark history of Socialist's policies was repeating in the here and now."

Chapter
26

I remember my grandfather telling me that "to be of value, spies and moles must be highly placed with access to classified information. Personal charm, cunning, courage, imagination, intelligence, risk-taking, and dull persistence are all valuable attributes."

Frank, I said, "I recommend that you read Kalugin's book. Oleg Kalugin, a KGB General, exposed the incredibly successful infiltration of Communists in American organizations in his book *Spymaster: My 32 Years in Intelligence and Espionage Against the West*. Kalugin was head of KGB operations, the NKVD's successor following a name change in the United States for many years.

"Disenchanted with Communism, he defected to the United States and became a citizen in 2003."

Frank had not heard of General Kalugin. So, I provided a brief background of the general.

"Early in his career, Kalugin worked undercover as a journalist while attending Columbia University in New York City as a Fulbright Scholar. He conducted espionage and influence operations as a Radio Moscow correspondent with the United Nations. He was a master spy in his own right, although he certainly had the spy gene in him. His father was an NKVD officer.

"He ingratiated himself to everyone he came into contact with, in the United States. He's a smooth talker and an even better listener. He also has plenty of guts. Most importantly, he's a terrific salesman and always willing to help anyone. Nobody had a bad word to say about him: in fact, he was a well-liked and admired person.

"His reach was deep and wide. He posed as a diplomat and met with Senator Mike Mansfield, William Fulbright, Mark Hatfield, Eugene McCarthy, and George McGovern. He spoke with Senator Robert Kennedy in the senator's office. He and his fellow spies did not attempt to recruit the senators, but they eagerly tried to recruit the senator's staff members.

"While in Washington, the general had good success in recruiting spies and moles: foreign diplomats and sources in the military as well as the Central Intelligence Agency.

"Some people were entrapped to work for the KGB. This was the case with a valuable diplomatic asset in Washington, a woman from a major European country. She was recruited using sex and romance.

"His most fruitful agent was a top diplomat from a Western European country. He provided diplomatic cables, top-secret reports, and even correspondence with the American State Department. Kalugin received the material following prearranged meetings in the halls of the old National Press Building. The foreign diplomat betrayed his country—not for money, nor because he was compromised, nor due to ego. He did it for ideological motives!

"A military intelligence officer—an Army colonel—and a retired Navy nuclear submarine captain were soon working for Kalugin. One did it because he was greedy for money, and the other because his ego was hurt since he was not promoted to admiral.

"NATO and other western intelligence services were also penetrated. This provided an excellent opportunity to plant disinformation and confuse our enemies.

"Kalugin's access reached into almost all categories of influential American people. As part of his journalist cover, he met with a wide variety of celebrities, some of which were comfortable in left-leaning political circles. He met with Eleonor Roosevelt, Edward R. Morrow, Shelley Winters, and Natalie Wood, to name a few."

"Many other agents of influence that worked for the NKVD suggested interfering in US elections to secure entry into the Senate and Congress, then ensuring the direction of and influencing American politics."

The mainstream media is incredibly powerful, my friend. I said to Frankie, "It was just like the years leading America into the Second World War. Then, the manipulation of American opinion through covert propaganda was tested in the National Press Building. Many Americans protested that the media was secretly intervening in elections as part of a campaign to bring the United States into World War II and help the Soviet Union.

"Using TASS, the Russian news agency, as cover, Soviet intelligence made the recruitment of American journalists a high priority. Soviet agents of influence were also talent spotters, like João had told my grandfather.

"Journalists were valued as sources because Moscow believed that they possessed insider information. And they were not too far off the mark," I said.

Kalugin wrote that "I. F. Stone, a politically progressive American investigative journalist and writer, claimed to present an objective account of the Soviet Union while secretly working for the NKVD. The NKVD recruited Walter Lippmann's personal secretary as an agent. Lippmann was an influential writer, reporter, and political commentator.

"The reach of the NKVD into the government of Franklin Delano Roosevelt is alarming. The Soviet intelligence agency recruited Harry Dexter White as an agent. White's job in FDR's cabinet was that of Assistant Secretary of the Treasury. Moscow knew firsthand where American finances were directed. Equally alarming was the work of Lauchlin Currie on behalf of the Soviets. Currie, FDR's economic advisor, betrayed his country when he told his NKVD handlers that the United States was on the verge of braking Soviet secret codes. The Soviets quickly changed their secret messaging. The United States was now left in the dark and looked for new ways to penetrate Soviet diplomatic cables. A lot of money, work, and time had been wasted."

At first Frank did not believe a word I said. He could not believe that Americans would betray their country.

I told Frank that the "intelligence, spy literature" is enormous. I recommended that he read *The Sword and the Shield: The Mitrokhin Archive and the Secret History of the KGB*, *The Mitrokhin Archive II: The KGB in the World*, both books by Christopher Andrews. "The list of books is long," I said.

One book in particular should send chills down your spine. "Kim Philby wrote *My Silent War: The Autobiography of a Spy*. Philby was a British intelligence officer and a double agent for the Soviet Union. Philby rose through the ranks and came incredibly close to becoming the head of the British Intelligence Service, MI6. Philby started his double life of patriot and spy as a freelance journalist."

It made me think, have government, intelligence agencies, law enforcement agencies, the media, science, education, and so many other agencies of influence been penetrated by our adversaries? If we were penetrated by Communists so many years ago, why would we not be penetrated today, when modern technology makes everything so much easier?

Already one former director of an intelligence agency admitted that, while a young man, he had voted for the Communist Party of the United States of America. After this revelation, one must ask the question, how deep have our intelligence agencies been penetrated by our enemies?

Is loyalty a lost virtue? In today's political atmosphere the Democratic Party and their Socialist and Progressive allies are bound by loyalty. Once a set of talking points are approved, no one deviates from them no matter what. They all march in cadence and the mainstream media repeats their message throughout the day ensuring the message is not forgotten. The same cannot be said of the Republican Party.

What if a former Republican Cabinet member turned against the hand that fed him, because his huge egos were hurt. The experts that serve the president in those high positions know that they serve only at the president's pleasure. They can be dismissed at any time.

What if a dishonorable and cowardly former advisor turned against his president when he was fired because his neo-conservative methods clashed with those of the president? Perhaps he is really like the camel with its head under the tent gathering information. Like Jacob wearing a rough goat skin on his arm to fool his blind and trusting father to receive his father's blessing. What if the advisor pretended to wear conservative skin to deceive his peers in government? That would be an act of complete dishonor and proof of someone lacking good morals.

When I really think about it, it is not the people already identified as "Left "or "Liberal" that worry me. It is the ones lurking freely and undetected in the deep corridors of government, media, and other influential positions. They are talented and useful spies and moles who are seldom detected, and the very best are not even suspected. They are the ones with real power, pulling strings to influence our national policies.

Frank you know you don't have to go spy school to learn all about spying and its consequences. There are plenty of unclassified literature on the subject easily accessible in your local library or bookstore. All you have to do is take the time to read about it.

Chapter
27

Frank, I said, "one thing we can all agree about politics is that it is never static—neither the good times nor the bad times last. Like in nature, it follows a cycle of growth and decay. Politicians know that process; they also know that despite their cleverness, they are not immune to that cycle. Another political axiom we can predict is that whenever something appears to be at the very top, you can be sure its demise already started.

"The best that we can do is live a moral life with the will to live within our means. Not desire too much, be self-sufficient, and do no harm. To accept that we are only on this earth for a short time."

"The Socialists do not own one single chromosome of virtue. It just does not appear in their DNA. They willingly fail to distinguish between truth and falsehood. They attack the opposition when they are having dinner at a restaurant, when walking down the streets, and at college campuses. They even have representatives in Congress that encourage acts of civil disobedience.

"It is our choice between good and evil that determines character, and not our opinion about good or evil. The Socialist threat is real and dangerous.

"Only Socialists deliberate about cyclical occurrences, like drought and rain, hot and cold. They know those things cannot be affected by men. They create political mirages to advance their goals. Incredibly, so many people fall for their magic. They think it is good to deceive when, in reality, it is not good at all. We should deliberate about things that are in our control and reachable by work and by action, not those occurrences beyond our control."

I told Frank that there are times when I admire Socialist discipline. "No doubt about it, the Socialists manage their business exceedingly well. They select a goal and consider how and by what means it must be achieved. Should there be several options to obtain it, they proceed with the path that will attain it most easily. It does not matter how much hate and discontent they cause. Once a course of action is approved, there is no turning back.

I could not get one thought out of my mind. Why is it that powerful people often get away with crimes?

If a mole makes his way into the government corridors, he will undoubtedly be in a position to promote chaos. Who or what organization is behind the curtain that ensures corrupt politicians continue walking free?

A crime was committed by a powerful person, yet this person still walks free. The country's premier law enforcement bureau did absolutely nothing to expose her amateurism or deliberate behavior in exposing national secrets. What is more, this former government official was protected by powerful allies in law enforcement, the intelligence community, and the justice department.

This powerful person is living proof that there are two sets of justice in our country. One set is for the powerful and the other set is for the rest of us.

Any other person with a Top Secret security clearance that hid a classified server somewhere in their home would have lost their security clearance and charged with a crime, perhaps even treason.

When an individual can get away with such actions, it can only mean one thing—they are untouchable. The law cannot touch them because they are unique, unlike the rest of us.

This stinking onion needed peeling, but could not be peeled because too many influential politicians, journalists, businessmen, military leadership, and key personnel in law enforcement, intelligence community, State Department, and Justice Department could be exposed in the coverup. People would go to jail. We all imagined that the law is equal to all people. Unfortunately, we all know that there is one set of law for the rich and powerful, and another set for everyone else.

Chapter
28

I thought how evil is entirely confined within our country. It is domestic. It is internal. Each citizen must cure it as best we can. The ambition of the 2016 Democratic Party run at the presidency was so reckless and colossal it might one day become a menace to our country, our Republic.

To remove all obstacles to power, forgive all debts, seize all property, and divide the spoils among their followers is not the way to win the hearts and minds of hard-working Americans.

As far as I can tell it became necessary to bind the conspirators even closer. Make them swear in blood; no one will talk, no one will ever leave the cabal. If anyone should be called on to answer questions, always deny, deny, deny everything.

Some politicians and their protectors did not find it challenging to lie in the service of political expediency. How was anyone to know that government spies worked on their behalf? As the old saying goes, "fish rots from the head down."

There is something rotten in Washington when the leadership of the Intelligence Community, the FBI, and the Judicial Departments work to provide cover and protect the guilty. Here precedence is manufactured by which a demagogue reaches out to the people and threatened to dispose of any challenger.

In a city like Washington, DC that knows all and conceals nothing, it is hard to believe that one could be so reckless unless there was already in place someone or something that provided top cover. That person must have felt "bulletproof" from any incoming rounds. How else could the Department of Justice grant immunity to the lawyer who destroyed 30,000 emails requested by Congress?

The deputy assistant director of the counterintelligence division and the special counsel to Deputy Director of an intelligence agency collaborated to promote doubt regarding the legitimacy of the president-elect. The two senior officers had a habit of communicating online, texts, and email. They were close associates. Sometimes, while online, they exchanged sensitive information. As security-trained professionals, they should have known better than to continue this practice. Perhaps they also felt untouchable and were not afraid of consequences. We will never know for sure.

When the former intelligence director was to testify before Congress, the same two senior officer's email revealed that they muddled the Director's congressional testimony. Moles from a previous administration, did everything they could to stop the duly elected president from promoting his Capitalist policies, which are in conflict with previous "Globalist" administration policies.

This was no dream I was experiencing, but a nightmare. This stinking onion is so large that it will take years to peel, and maybe it will never be wholly peeled. What is needed to do the job is courageous journalists willing to unravel the Gordian knot that is the classified home server, the destroyed 30,000 emails, Russia collusion, Ukraine quid pro quo, bribery, and impeachment inquiry.

The flight attendant announced that we would be landing in twenty minutes. Cabin preparation for the landing at Ninoy Aquino International Airport in Manila commenced without delay.

As we started our descent to the airport, I thought about how close the United States had come to a coup d'état, and how the 2020 election will be the most consequential in our country's history. It will be a fight for individual freedom versus group shackles. It will be a duel between Socialism and Capitalism!

PART
3

Chapter

29

As I walked around the hotel room putting away my clothes, I thought about the conversation with Frank.

The 2020 Presidential election is the most important election in my lifetime. The Globalist came incredibly close to taking over our country in 2016. All the current democrat candidates for the presidency are weak. One candidate during his campaign stops does not remember if he is in Iowa or Michigan and constantly confuses his wife for his sister. The person that matters in that presidential ticket is the vice-president. He is only a placeholder. The other front runner is an old Socialist-Democrat. What does that mean? It just does not make sense.

The Republican Party is the stepchild of the mainstream media. It is set aside and punished at every opportunity. Generally beaten at the polls, in 2016, the justice of their principles and the deceitful practices of the previous administration convinced the American people that a change was needed.

In the 2016 election, Republicans defeated Democrats upon the most palpable issue that was ever presented to the American people and one that they understood the best—Socialism is un-American!

From 2009 to 2016, the Republican Party was in the minority and the Democratic Party in the majority and consistently gaining more power. Then the unthinkable happened. The leading Democratic candidate lost the election despite having influential supporters on both sides of the political aisle, the media, and government officials.

A businessman with zero political experience, beat the Democratic candidate. On the one hand, there was a candidate with political experience and an army of supporters. She was indebted to several people and organizations that could pull her strings to get her to do what they ordered. On the other hand, the businessman did not owe anything to anyone or organization. He was free to put his policies into effect, not the policies of the "Swamp."

The imperfect statesman qualities of the president-elect and fictional collusion with an adversary nation were the reasons for his removal from office, said the mainstream media and the opposition party. However, the president proved to have a steel spine. A year into his presidency, he proved to be a quick political learner. For the time being, Capitalism churns the nation's economic engine, but the specter of Socialism is in the shadows. We are but an election away from becoming Socialists!

For the Democrats, Socialists, Globalists, or Progressives having lost the election, must have been disheartening. Everybody, at some point, loses an election. The winning side is happy with their triumph. It has been this way since the very first election that gave us President George Washington. The problem is that the present-day Democrats cannot accept the election of the current president. They lament the election results, but that does not give them the right to raise a hand against the Constitution, which in my mind makes the "Democrat" atmosphere thick with treason.

I settled down in my hotel room and started to write down ideas regarding the 2020 election. I thought about João and my grandfather and their discussion regarding agents of influence, disinformation, useful idiots, and agent provocateurs.

We often hear that the Socialists and the media "hate" our president. I think this is simply wrong. The Left would "hate" any man or woman that had defeated their anointed would-be president.

As it happened, the anointed one was her own worst enemy. She did not work hard enough to win; she expected the throne to be handed over to her in January 2017.

However, when a candidate, as the Republican candidate, sees the possibility of winning, he works extra hard. The president won because he is a hard worker, intelligent, and possesses high energy. She lost because she is lazy and has low energy. He works for the American people. She would have been indebted to the Globalists. Our president is not indebted to lobbyist or anyone else.

"Not to know what happened before one was born is always to be a child"–Cicero. I realized that in confronting the Socialist movement that gentile tactics and strategy ethically founded would no longer work. The Socialists and their allies must be fought using the very same tactics and strategy they currently employ. It was time to look at the battlefield from a different point of view if there is any chance of success.

The Socialists are pushing the Democratic Party more and more to the Left. They do not care how they take over the reign of power as long as they take it. It does not matter how much suffering they cause.

Socialists know little about what is best for the people's happiness, but much about destroying human dignity. Their beliefs are thick in treason, and they are willing to destroy the very country that has allowed them to thrive.

They know that the poor will suffer much, but they see it as a means to justify the end, even when they claim to be the champion of the little people. Their theorem is that people are already suffering, so a bit more suffering cannot do any more harm.

Then we have the aftereffects of redistribution of wealth. People snatch the blessings of others for themselves taking everything, they can for their own benefit. Then jealousy and hatred grow, and the community ceases to exist in harmony. There you have the spark necessary to start class warfare, a destructive fire stoked by hate, resentment, and jealousy. It splits the country into two distinct camps, making it easier to trigger a revolt from within that will make the country weaker. As João said: "Socialists want to blow up the world!"

We are facing a humorless, dark, soulless, godless cloud that was born in the East and is rapidly heading west to the United States—Socialism! It is a political system and philosophy founded on shaky grounds and has wholly failed wherever it has ruled. What does that tell us about the Socialist leadership? If this movement succeeds in taking charge of our country, then sorrow and despair will dawn, and a new Dark Age will emerge.

The American military is the best in the world, never losing on the field of battle. Its only loss, Vietnam, can be directly traced to weak politicians and civilian dissenters hell-bent on destroying our country. Indeed, the worst difficulties from which we suffer today do not come from without; they come from within. They come from the acceptance of immoral and unethical doctrines by a large proportion of our politicians. The new, unfettered drive to allow abortion even after a child is born. Look at the new Virginia law as an example. They have nothing to offer but a vague form of Internationalism that today has a more common name: Globalism.

The US cannot lose from without—adversaries, foreign and domestic, know that fact. The only way the US can be defeated is from within. One strategy to destroy the United States is to bankrupt it. Socialists promote the redistribution of wealth. Government would provide for every person in America several thousands of dollars a year to spend even if they do not work. The Green New Deal, the brainchild of a twenty-nine-year-old politician from New York. Free education, healthcare, housing, and food for illegal immigrants. The giveaways proposed by some in Congress and those "Democrats" running for president, if successful, will accomplish the total and complete downfall of the United States. The best government system devised by man and gifted to us by our Founding Fathers.

At the start of twenty-first century, America suffered the 9/11 attacks. New York and Washington DC saw two of its most potent symbols under siege: The Twin Towers and the Pentagon. In the fields of Pennsylvania, Americans took matters into their hands, and downed determined terrorists hell-bent into crashing a highjacked passenger aircraft into another symbol of power, perhaps the Capitol Building. If you do not resist evil, then you are helping it, and should outright admit it. The United States fought back against the scourge of radical Islamic terrorists.

The terrorist attacks of September 11, 2001 slowed down the "Globalist" movement in United States as more and more Americans rediscovered patriotism. Somehow the patriotic resurgence had to be downplayed and the fake kumbaya "Globalist" movement restored. Less than ten years after the horrific terrorist attack by Islamists, a bolt from the blue restarted the "Globalist" engine.

In 2009, an American politician more interested in becoming a world's president became the President of the United States. The Globalist politician apologized to the world at large. Never mind all the American blood and treasure lost in Afghanistan and Iraq. He did not see America as an exceptional city shining on a hill. Instead, America was just like any other country of the broader Earth.

The apologist-in-chief went about the globe, especially in the Muslim world, atoning for America's sins in Afghanistan, Iraq, and other radical Islamic global hotspots. He succeeded in dividing the country even more than it already was.

Years later, a president of the United States is having a conversation with the then president of Russia. This was a troubling conversation that should have raised many questions concerning our president, but he did not have to worry, he had mainstream media top cover. Instead, the incident was underreported or entirely ignored by the media.

The president said to the Russian president "after the coming election, I will have 'more flexibility' in dealing with issues."

The conversation is caught in an open microphone. Basically, our president was asking the Russian president for time. Please do not bring up the question of missile defense system while I am running for re-election.

Imagine if the current president had said those words. They media would have accused him of treason and impeachment would quickly follow.

The facts are that it was the previous Democratic administration that appeased Russia by withdrawing missile defense from the United States' central European allies, Poland and the Czech Republic. It was under that same administration Russia annexed Crimea, invaded Ukraine, and provided military aid and intervention in Syria. Facts are hard to ignore even when they are true.

Under the previous administration, lawless acts were committed throughout the United States without repercussion from law enforcement or the Justice Department. Cities like Chicago experienced some of the highest rates of murder ever recorded in the United States, even though the city has the strictest gun laws in the land. In Chicago, only bad guys own firearms.

Baltimore was set ablaze. "Let the people have their way," declared the liberal mayor. The city was a bonfire for days. First responders handcuffed by their "leadership" could not stop the rioting and looting. The city burned, and lawbreaking continued unabated.

Socialists like to call these unlawful acts "social justice." Socialist justice is injustice. By the way, whenever there is a modifier before justice, remember it has nothing to do with justice at all, instead it is a newly discovered Socialist political movement.

Civilization rests directly on coercion, some people claim. What holds a society together is not the cop, but the goodwill of the average person. However, that goodwill is powerless unless the policeman is there to enforce the laws. The fact is, whoever is not on the side of the police officer is on the side of the criminal.

It takes strong leadership to push back the destructive tide facing our country today. On the Left, we only have dark and angry mediocre leaders attempting to allow the deadly Socialist wave to engulf the entire country. The Right, for the most part, also has weak leaders, some of which are Left-leaning and have infiltrated the Right's leadership circle.

Socialists stand up and frankly admit that our Constitution, the very best document to guide a country devised by man, requires change now. The Speaker of the House reports to the American people that the president must be impeached to protect our Constitution. Still, her party is ready to make changes to the Constitution as soon as they take power. They look to take power legitimately or by cheating.

For example, removing the electoral college and only having the popular vote matter in the presidential election. What about protecting the Constitution, Madam Speaker? What about keeping the Constitution intact for perpetuity? Socialists claim that the Constitution is a living organism, and it is time to change it!

Thankfully, the delegates to the Constitutional Convention realized that in most elections, the large states would dominate the popular vote. That system would make the election less fair to the smaller states. The electoral college is a fair system that allows all states, large and small, an equal voice in selecting a president.

The question today is whether in a free country, the faction, the minority has the right to break up the government whenever they choose? What if an inchoate wing of Socialist fire-eaters succeeds in winning the presidency, Congress, and the Senate, then, what are we, the hard-working American people to do? One thing is for sure: should that scenario come true: freedom—gone, and individual liberty—gone!

The middle class, the American working class, in many cases, fail to recognize that the Socialists are carrying out a social experiment at their expense. Those Socialist politicians carrying the experiment do not know what it is like to go to work every day and what it takes to feed and raise a family.

The "Left's" new world, however, is being revealed—whoever opposes Socialism is also ipso facto stupid and a deplorable.

It does not matter that the vast majority of American citizens, natural-born or naturalized, were bred under the Stars and Stripes. We celebrate the Fourth of July with pride. We admire our national emblems as markers of safety and prosperity to us, our children, and our children's children. Now the Socialist fire-eaters are hell-bent on destroying all those national symbols. They aim to replace them with Globalist symbology reminiscent of the "worker's paradise—Internationalism" of the Russian Revolution of 1917.

This faction takes a hostile attitude towards our American flag; sometimes they burn it and step on it. The American flag is a great symbol of freedom, a symbol that must be respected by all Americans no matter whether Democrat or Republican. But the fire-eaters, the Democrats' mad rebellious faction, must be held accountable for their divisive platform engineered to destroy the country from the inside out.

Chapter

30

Above anything else, people want the truth. The problem is that one cannot fight the Socialists with reason or conventionality. They are incredibly flexible, and like the phoenix, they continually rise time and time again from their ashes!

Socialists and their allies instinctively know how to turn the truth into a falsehood. It is all about their will to power. The takeover of the United States of America by any means.

Today the American people have good jobs and are working themselves up the ladder of success. The media omits, underreports, or modifies the excellent news to fit their Socialist agenda. They look for storm clouds where there are none. It is as if they want our country to fail.

Why is it that so many people believe in a lie that could not fool even a child? They hold on to it and repeat it in defiance to all evidence to the contrary. The question that no one is asking should be—are these constant investigations designed to uncover wrongdoings by the new Republican administration? Or is the intention to cover up the wrongdoings of the previous Democratic administration?"

Saul D. Alinsky wrote *Rules for Radicals: A Pragmatic Primer for Realistic Radicals* in 1971, a book dedicated to Lucifer. He was a man envious of everyone else's success with a peculiar personal loathing of American democracy. In the book, he described the meaning of power and how to use it. It appears to me that this book is the Socialist's guide to taking power.

Alinsky wrote, "go outside the knowledge of the enemy and make the enemy live up to its own rules. We do not have to follow our regulations. Additionally, ridicule the enemy; keep the pressure on the enemy, and if you push a negative hard and deep enough, it will break through as fact. But the most important rule is to pick a target, freeze it, personalize it, and polarize it."

Exactly the practice utilized against the current president. Why attack the current president? Because he fights for the American people. He is an American and not a Globalist!

Alinsky combines hatred with fear. He enjoys the pleasure of hatred, which is how this frightened man promotes himself for the failure that was his life. So, the more he fears, the more he hates. Readers remember that the devil is a liar!

The president is a successful Capitalist, finally bringing back prosperity to America, and a real enemy to the Socialist cause. He engages them by unconventional means. You see, the president, unlike the previous Republican presidents, fights back! This personal trait angers the mainstream media and Socialists.

How can anyone fault the man for fighting back, for standing for his rights when a flood of lies is hurled against him on a daily basis.

He is his best marketer. He bypasses the biased network news with skillful use of technology—Twitter! That's how he gets his good news message to the people, which infuriated the media to no end.

The media will announce and repeat lies, half-truths, and innuendos mixed with partial truths, leaving the entire country completely confused and wondering what to believe and what to discard. Even the "fair and balanced" network has its fair share of anchors, pundits, and guest speakers that are Socialists dressed in conservative clothing. They are like the camel with its nose under the tent, taking in, sniffing all that is being said.

Hippocrates said, 'First, do no harm.' Socialists disregard this cautionary phrase; instead, they are out to destroy the best Constitution ever created—a document written by geniuses. The United States is lucky that these geniuses all happened to live at the same time in history. They worked with each other. It took years of intellectual debate until they got it right. How blessed is the United States of America to have had these tremendous common sense and rational minds working together to create the US Constitution?

Now the country is faced with angry, humorless, non-intellectual, pessimist losers who look forward to the day they can rewrite the Constitution—forget the Bill of Rights.

In America, it did not matter what religion one practiced. Neighbors helped each other out. There was peace and harmony in most neighborhoods.

Now, two congresswomen, one from Minnesota and the other from Michigan, are rabid anti-Semites. Their hatred for the Jew has no bounds. They fail to recognize that if some Jews succeed in obtaining the more advantageous and lucrative positions, it is because of strong family ties, belief in the almighty, discipline, love for higher education, and excellent work ethic. Qualities that any group of people can pursue.

We have a senator from a small state who claims to be a Democratic Socialist. Talk about oxymorons! He is a Bolshevik, a relic out of central casting from the 1917 Russian Revolution. A "Socialist" who has personally benefitted from Capitalism. He has a personal wealth of about $2 million and owns three homes. What a hypocrite!

A man that cannot criticize Communist Cuba and Venezuela. Who honeymooned in Moscow, when Moscow was the capital of the Union of Soviet Socialists Republics. He even praised the Communist country.

By the way, why is an American politician honeymooning in Moscow? Was he working for the Communists? Did he get training on how to secretly communicate with his Communist handlers?

Now he wants to bring that failed system to the United States of America.

Here we have the politician who would roll over for Moscow at the first opportunity.

Real Socialists reject private property ownership. The senator has significant wealth, yet he begs for more money from everyone so that he can redistribute it—a man ready to spend other people's money as long as he keeps his own wealth safe and sound. He is a man that finishes every angry sentence by extending his right arm and tapping out Morse Code with his fingers for emphasis. Morse Code is the technology he best understands—1917 technology!

The would-be author of Medicare for All is alive today because our present healthcare system saved his life. He did not have to wait in line when he suffered a medical emergency far away from his home state. Instead, the doctors and nurses immediately admitted him into a hospital, prepared the operating room with all the latest technological instruments, and placed a stent to open up his arteries. He is alive because of our excellent healthcare system the very system that saved his life and the system he wants to destroy.

Medicare-for-all forgets about the people that have paid into that system for so many years. Like the Green New Deal that promises economic security for those unwilling to work and the elimination of flatulent cows. It is as if these ideas are made to attract attention on something that is so "out there" that it just does not make sense. Maybe the design is to keep lawmakers from focusing on real issues that affect each and every citizen each and every day. Whatever the reason, these ideas just create more and more division among the people.

I ask, "Why would anyone trust a politician whose initials are BS?"

Chapter
31

As I look back at what my grandfather taught me and my research, it seems to me that in 2020, the current Left political movement resembles the Marxist movement of the 1920s and 1930s. Their goal is to make everyone dependent on the government. They invite people into their clever trap. They offer wide and welcome doors with promises impossible to keep, but that led only to misery and self-destruction. The problem is that it is nearly impossible to break free of the Socialist's chains once they are in place.

When a myth such as Socialism is widely accepted, people will, unfortunately, discover little or no correlation with relationships that do not exist. One thing is book Socialism and another is living in Socialism.

Today the country is being held together by the United States Constitution. This magnificent document is the only barrier keeping the Socialists from taking power. They are looking for ways to remove the roadblocks that prevent them from "legally" assuming power.

The phrase "in good faith" loses meaning when the highly developed technique of lying to oneself is formed. When self-deception becomes the norm, it is no longer an excuse.

The Socialist lied and never knew that he had lied, and when it was pointed out to him, he said that lies were beautiful and smiled. Today's Socialists are wiser, more skillful, and more treacherous in their ways. Trial and error mastered the pros and cons of their deceitful art over a long period of time.

It reminds me of a journalist's behavior, as described by João, to my grandfather, in 1940. Their task was to mount a series of provocative operations intended to give the false impression that Capitalism was evil and Socialism good.

When a group, a fiercely loyal club, sets a goal, and they dominate the airwaves, they are at the forefront of reviews and write the majority of serious books, then, they control the media and public opinion. They instruct ordinary people how to think on how to behave.

They fill newspapers and airwaves with truths, half-truths, and lies with no intentions of being fair and or balanced.

It is as if a secret faction, that is, a portion of the journalists' club are members of the Socialist movement. They meet in secret and decide what policies the club should promote. When they put forth their ideas in the open, the sheer strength of their arguments usually persuades the innocent public and the result is that many follow their instructions blindly.

Their misinformed following is comprised of disordered enthusiasts, believers in anything, and everything. Habitual followers of the latest deceitful messiah.

I decided to do a little research regarding the journalist's past behavior, and what I discovered was alarming. It turns out that Soviet Union intelligence services targeted the White House, Congress, State Department, CIA, FBI, Pentagon, top scientific research centers, think tanks, and major corporations. A huge task to take on, but one that could be taken in small bites.

Intelligence agencies hire the best and the brightest men and women the country has to offer—patriots. Unfortunately, intelligence agencies also employ vain, villainous, and ignorant men and women, making it difficult to identify the greatest blockheads and the greatest rogue among the spies.

It is a fact that a former director of the US best-known intelligence agency once voted for the Communist Party of the United States of America; this revelation should come as a warning to true Americans that the most dangerous threat to our way of life does not come from without but from within.

If Socialism, ever takes hold in the United States, this is what we can expect: lousy homes that all look the same, bad cars, inadequate medical healthcare, lousy electrical power, faulty heating, scarce and lousy food, horrible art, more drug and alcohol abuse, more crime, rise of black markets, more hatred, more envy, more poverty, and the list can go on and on.

All we have to do is look back at the standard of living of the Russian people under Communism. Or if you desire to be more contemporary, look at what is happening in Venezuela and what already happened to the Cuban people—misery!

If Socialism takes over, there will be two classes of people. The wealthy Socialist nomenklatura and the poor. The middle class will disappear.

The economic class that will complain the most will be upper-middle class that helped wittingly or unwittingly the Socialist train. They are digging their own misery graves because they were duped by the very best liars this world has ever developed—Socialists and presently Globalists. They were duped by "social justice" claims and Political Correctness. They eagerly herd themselves to the slaughterhouse ready to be a sacrificial offering to the Socialists gods. They are completely blind even when their eyes are wide open.

The upper-middle class will be shamed for their financial success. If they have one or more homes, they will be told to give up all their homes to the government except the one they choose to live in. Why should homes remain empty while there are plenty of homeless families ready to occupy them?

What to expect if the Socialists win the 2020 election. The abolition of the electoral college, a tax rate of 70% or higher. Even if you taxed the wealthiest Americans at a 100% rate it would not be enough money to cover all the handouts the Socialists would give. In time, an equally oppressive tax will reach down to the middle class since they should also pay their "fair share." The only people that do not pay their "fair share" would be the politicians and unelected government administrators. They do not produce anything, they only take.

All of this is in addition to doubling down on their support for open borders. That allows any group of people to come into the country and receive benefits: free healthcare, free welfare, free college tuition, and more. Why will these illegals be given everything for free? Simple answer. It has nothing to do with caring for our fellow human beings. You see, one day they will all be legal and vote Socialist!

These are the same people who think that they can secure for themselves self-composed glory by fraud and cunning speech. However, they are wildly mistaken. Deceit can only last for a short time. A lie, in politics or family matters, cannot be covered forever. The truth always rises to the top. Motivated by opposition to Capitalism and a desire to help the Socialist movement, many reporters volunteered to serve as clandestine operatives for the cause. They drove manufactured tales of infidelity, thievery, and sexual abuse, for example. Reporters included those embedded in newspapers, radio, online news, the TV that reported on false news generated by intelligence operatives. They did it because they knew that by shaping public opinion, then there was a chance to change the course of their country's history.

Chapter
32

G od is slow to anger. Socialists are quick to anger. The conspiracy takes us to the center of Socialists political scheming from the twentieth to the twenty-first century. Its conventions, its conflicts, its half-truths coupled with lies, its controversies, and how they plotted to reverse a fair election—a coup d'état.

A cabal of intelligence executives gathered much needed intelligence. They were like double agents hoping to entangle the president-elect with a fabricated dossier designed to take him down and replace him with their chosen leader.

Usually, the FBI run its intelligence operations from one of their field offices. This plot against the president was run from the seventh floor, the leadership floor of the Hoover Building. This was done to have complete operational secrecy and control.

Hopefully, one day soon, this cabal will be exposed for their seditious acts. It is to be seen who talks and where the blame lies; how far up the chain of command knew about the treasonous act, and when did they know?

The president listened to a sham impeachment, a blistering and well-orchestrated attack with no legitimate articles of impeachment. There was no treason, bribery, or other high crimes and misdemeanors. Instead, phony impeachment articles were made up by lying congressional Democrats.

It was a marvelous mixture of fury and anger. Back and forth went the Democrats in an attempt to have a successful coup d'état.

They mounted a treasonous sting operation to expose the conspirators in the new administration. The mainstream media, for whatever reason, probably for their survival, backed the doubtful process, with false evidence and broadcasted it as truth.

But it is always worth trying to read and understand what is behind the mainstream media version. It is important to remember that it is not always what is said but how it is said.

When listening to many of today's journalists, one would think that they came down from heaven by immaculate conception. Pure as spring water rolling down the mountain into stream. Who has a picture of the private lives of these wholesome journalists? Do we know what they do behind closed doors?

The commission designated to look for evidence of collusion between Russia and the President of the United States of America found zero evidence, after more than two years of looking under every possible political and personal rock.

Dejected with no conspiracy findings, the Socialists best hope to derail the President required another angle of attack. A new set of investigations led members of Congress from liberal New York and California.

Democrats in conjunction with the mainstream media will never allow for a formal inquiry. No corrupt politician would allow independent men to control an investigation whose result could be inflammatory.

Socialists are like a swarm of fire ants, attacking and destroying anyone that gets in their dishonorable way. For the 2020 election, they have assembled a team of attack ants that are running for president. They repeatedly spew their verbal venom against the standing president. A barrage of slander against a president who has provided the best economy for all citizens to enjoy. African Americans, Whites, Hispanics, and Women are benefitting from his economic boom as never before in the country's history.

A thinking person with the ability to conduct critical thinking knows that Socialism is but one step away from Communism. Our country is in peril of being taken over by envious, deceitful, angry, godless people.

Aviation advances have come a long way from the time my grandfather traveled to Manila in 1940. Air transportation is considered the safest way to travel these days. A passenger can go to the farthest destinations in comfort and most importantly in safety.

Unfortunately, Socialism is still a plague in our society. The Socialist leadership is hell-bent in forcing that pessimistic political system throughout the globe. Modern air travel has improved the lives of all people while Socialism continues to deprive men and women from reaching their individual goals.

The United States of America is one legitimate election or one successful Democrat coup d'état from becoming another failed Socialist country.

Future elections will decide if the United States of America will remain so or become the People's States of America. Should the Socialists win, it will be the beginning of a new terrible dark age.

Socialism is truly the Walking Dead!

Epilogue

In February of 2020 I spent a couple of weeks in Beaufort with an old college friend and his family. His house was located in the historic district. It was the perfect size not too big or small. It was a beautiful antebellum house. Like the ones in the movies. It had been passed down from generation to generation for over one hundred and fifty years

I had not been back since my grandfather passed away 1999. My grandfather's funeral mass was held in MCRD's chapel. Then our small family attended the burial in Arlington Cemetery his final resting place. I was impressed and proud by the number of retired military and intelligence community personnel that attended the ceremony.

I could not help and think of my grandfather's 1940 trip to Manila. It dawned on me how ingenious Juan Trippe had been in selecting the route from mainland USA to China. Each island on the route was fought over by the United States and Japan during the war. Hawaii, Midway, Wake, Guam and the Philippine Islands were all sights where the two powerful nations fought.

For Trippe, the islands on the way to China provided a safe and economical way to travel over the vast Pacific Ocean.

For Japan, the islands were much more than that. They were strategic bases of operation to safeguard the Japanese Island from invasion.

My musing came to an end while standing in my friend's backyard. I heard a distant growl that grabbed my attention. I looked in the direction of the sound but saw absolutely nothing. The growl got deeper, throatier as it got closer to my location. A tiny speck in the sky was getting bigger and bigger as it seemed to be coming directly over me. Now in full view, I saw two Marine F-35 flying in formation as they made their approach to the Marine Air Base in Beaufort. They looked like manta rays. It must have been the angle to the aircraft because what I saw was a resembled flying wing, a Manta Ray flying the above the South Carolina sky instead of swimming in the Atlantic Ocean. When the warbirds passed overhead, I could not hold back my pride and admiration and gave a loud yell and said, "That's the sight and sound of freedom!"

During my Beaufort stay, I witnessed Marine F-35, F/A-18 and an occasional Air Force F-16 practice touch'n go at the Marine Air Base before heading out to the Atlantic to improve their skills at dogfighting.

Later that night as I got ready to go to bed, I wondered. "How much longer will that beautiful sight and sound of freedom last if any of the Democratic candidates wins the next election?" I could not help but think that they would drastically cut the defense budget to pay for the free giveaway they propose? I had a fitful night's sleep.

I drove the back routes to New York, avoiding I-95 and its insane traffic. Along the way I passed beautifully kept farms;

the family name proudly displayed. Small businesses dotted the landscape from South Carolina all the way to New York: gas stations, landscaping businesses, hi-tech support businesses, furniture and grocery stores, pet stores, homes for the elderly, automobile dealerships, in fact, to list the privately owned business that I saw would take the first ten chapters of *Moby Dick*.

Parents dropped off their kids at school and then went to work as doctors, nurses, salespeople, firefighters, and much more.

As I headed north, the Ford F-150s and Chevy Sierras traded the boats they were trailing for skimobiles and snow skis. The country was enjoying an economic growth spurt.

A sense of pride came over me. The United States of America was the richest and most successful country that ever existed. America was rich and prosperous because its people worked hard, they did not wait in line for government handouts. Americans are not Socialists.

Americans are individuals that want to be left alone while they search for the corner of happiness. Yet they gather at church or a community center to help the less fortunate. Americans are the most generous people in the world.

After a couple days of driving, I was back home. There is nothing like being in one's home and sleeping on your own bed. I slept incredibly well that night. I awoke in the same position I had fallen asleep; completely refreshed and energized knowing that American people will not surrender their liberty to government handouts. Instead, Americans believe in earning their keep.